Death of a

Blogger

A Lady Marjorie Snellthorpe Mystery
Novella

Dawn Brookes

Death of a Blogger

A Lady Marjorie Snellthorpe Mystery

Dawn Brookes

Oakwood Publishing

Paperback Edition 2021
Paperback ISBN: 978-1-913065-31-7
Copyright © DAWN BROOKES 2021
Cover Images adapted from Adobe Stock Images:
Amsterdam Landscape, Johnnyknez
Elderly lady with mobile phone, andrew_rybalko
Elderly lady in foreground, Good Studio
Cover Design: Dawn Brookes

Chapter 1

Lady Marjorie Snellthorpe flicked through an English copy of *The Times* newspaper while waiting for her friends to arrive from the airport. She wanted them to register with the tour guide together, but was also glad of the rest after a late night at the Theatre DeLaMar the evening before. She had flown into Amsterdam a day early to enjoy the sights and visit places she had been to with her late husband, Ralph, topping it off with dinner followed by a performance of *Fiddler on the Roof.*

A hullabaloo in the hotel lobby dragged her attention away from a news article about a government-led increased investment strategy for green energy. After lowering the newspaper and lifting her chin, she could just make out the back of a weighty woman wearing a fluorescent pink dress seriously clashing with her bright red hair. Just as Marjorie had the ruckus in view, someone bumped into her seat, sending her reading glasses flying off the side of the arm onto the floor.

"I'm so sorry," stuttered a tall, buxom woman who appeared to be in her early seventies. "I was distracted by the commotion over there and wasn't looking where I was going."

The woman's left hand covered her mouth. Marjorie retrieved her spectacles while noticing the woman's bright blue floral-patterned summer dress was cut low around the chest, and the documents in her right hand.

"No harm done," she closed the newspaper and folded it before turning her attention back towards the raised voice. Marjorie shook her head in dismay, hoping that by doing so she could shake away the glimmer of recognition at the voice doing the shouting. Shockwaves descended her spine. Marjorie hoped she was mistaken; she couldn't see the noisy woman clearly, but she could certainly hear her – along with everyone else in reception.

Surely not! Anyway, the woman she knew had grey hair.

"I DON'T CARE WHETHER YOU CAN FIND MY NAME ON YOUR LIST OR NOT! I've booked this trip and I'm going, whatever your printout says. Find me someone who knows what they're doing, won't you!"

The flustered young tour guide, her blonde hair tied back in a ponytail, stepped backwards as the older woman encroached on her personal space. She frantically scanned a list on a clipboard.

"Oh dear. I do hope she's not one of ours," remarked the woman who had bumped into Marjorie's chair. "I see from your luggage you're joining the Amsterdam to Budapest river cruise?"

Marjorie was still taking in the unravelling scene as it got nearer to the reception desk, along with the dreaded recognition of the woman causing the nuisance; she barely managed to respond to the lady who was awaiting her reply.

"Yes, I am. And looking forward to it, too. Marjorie Snellthorpe, how do you do?"

"Greta Mitchell. Nice to meet you." The woman smiled. *Somewhat forced*, thought Marjorie.

Greta helped herself to a chair opposite Marjorie. "I think I'll wait here until the disturbance dies down. Larry – that's my husband – should be along soon. He left his phone in the taxi; he's such a blundering idiot these days, doesn't seem at all focussed. I'm hoping the holiday will do him good. The concierge has had to call the driver back."

"Oh dear, how inconvenient." Marjorie was only half listening as the fracas at reception became louder again. Most people had stopped what they were doing and were staring disapprovingly at the vociferous woman causing the rumpus.

Another woman, wearing a pristine sky-blue suit with a tailored blouse similar to those of the young tour guide attempting to deal with the unseemly guest, appeared and took over. She was older, in her forties, and had an air of seniority.

"I'm terribly sorry, madam. If there's been a mistake, we'll sort it out. Come with me and let me ring head office to see if I can find out what's happened. Why don't you sit over here while I get this sorted?" Leading the troublesome woman away, she nodded to the younger woman to carry on as a crowd had gathered in a queue.

"Thank goodness that's settled. I can't be doing with troublesome people like her," said Greta.

"Mm," was all Marjorie could bring herself to say. She noticed people resume whatever it was they had been doing before the commotion started as if nothing had happened.

"Are you taking the cruise alone?" Greta forced Marjorie's head away from the disappearing cause of the trouble. Detecting a hint of disapproval in the other woman's tone, on closer inspection, Marjorie noticed tight lips and deep frown lines beneath a heavy layer of foundation.

"I do travel alone occasionally since my husband, Ralph, died, but on this trip, I have two young friends to accompany me."

"No family, then?"

Greta Mitchell was beginning to annoy Marjorie, but she answered politely. "I have a son who manages the family business, he and his wife live a few miles away from me. Rachel – one of the young women joining me – is like a granddaughter. We're very close… Ah, speaking of which, here they are." Marjorie was happy to see the beaming faces of her young friends heading straight for her. Rachel leaned down and had thrown her arms around her and kissed her cheek before Marjorie had time to stand up.

"Marjorie! It's wonderful to see you. Sorry we're late, Sarah was stopped and searched coming through customs. I've always said she looks like a criminal." Rachel's infectious laugh and wink made Marjorie feel all was well in the world again.

Sarah nudged her friend out of the way and kissed Marjorie on the other cheek. "What did I say about not telling anyone, Rachel Prince? You're terrible. Hello, Marjorie, it's lovely to see you. You're looking well."

"And I'm feeling well, dear. I'm not long back from taking a stroll around the markets and thought I'd wait for you before registering for the tour. I was just reading *The Times* before Mrs Mitchell here joined me." Marjorie beamed with pride as Rachel and Sarah introduced themselves to the wide-eyed, disapproving Greta Mitchell.

"Thank you for keeping our friend company. I'm Rachel, this is Sarah."

Greta took the outstretched hands, dropping them quickly. "What's that about being searched?"

"Oh, it was nothing." Rachel smiled at a red-faced Sarah before addressing Greta again. "Are you on the river cruise?"

"Yes. My husband and I are taking to the water for the first time. We usually holiday in the South of France. This is his choice." Marjorie picked up the disparaging tone again. "It's our Golden Wedding Anniversary."

"Wow! Congratulations," replied Rachel and Sarah in unison.

"Thank you, but it's not until Wednesday." Greta huffed before changing the subject. "You've just missed a dreadful argument between a fat woman and that young tour guide over there." Greta nodded towards the blonde woman checking in the guests. "They were going at it like a pair of alley cats when I arrived."

Marjorie felt the 'fat' woman, a rude term at the best of times, especially as the woman she was referring to wasn't much bigger than Greta herself, but she remained silent.

"Oh?" quizzed Rachel. "Anything we need to worry about?"

Marjorie's eyes warned Rachel off the topic. Her young friend could always read her. She shook her head slightly and Rachel took the hint.

"About time! Here's my husband at last," announced Greta, standing up.

A worried-looking sparrow-like man with a balding head looked up at his wife. "Panic over." He waved his phone in the air before placing it in the inside jacket pocket of his brown suit.

Without introducing them to her husband, Greta abruptly took his arm and hustled him towards the young guide. "Come along, Larry. I want to check in and get an early dinner booking. You have no idea what I've been through waiting for you. Please take more care in future…"

The apparently hen-pecked Larry meekly followed his wife towards the young tour guide, who smiled at them, revealing polished white teeth.

"Little and Large," chuckled Marjorie.

"I feel sorry for the poor man," said Sarah, who was always kind. Her hazel-green eyes trailed the couple momentarily before she took a seat next to Marjorie. "This is so exciting. I get to take a cruise where I'm the one being looked after for a change. Although being searched at the airport wasn't a brilliant start. And for your information, Rachel, I look nothing like a criminal."

"It is Amsterdam, my dear. They can't be too careful, you know. Anyway, let's hope you don't need looking after in hospital; I wouldn't want you having to make comparisons there," teased Marjorie. Sarah worked as a nurse on board a cruise ship owned by Queen Cruises, the same line that owned the river cruise vessel they would be joining the next morning. She and Rachel had originally met Marjorie on a cruise to the Mediterranean when Rachel had saved Marjorie's life. Sarah was Rachel's lifelong best friend and they had all become close over the past few years.

"And let's hope there are no murders," said Rachel.

"I suppose there has to be one downside. You know how I love to be your investigating assistant," laughed Marjorie.

Rachel giggled. "I can't believe you said that, Marjorie Snellthorpe."

"I can," said Sarah, giving Marjorie a disapproving frown.

The queue forming in front of the young guide lengthened and the more senior one joined her to assist with taking names and handing out information folders. There was no sign of the troublesome person from earlier.

"I think we should wait for the queue to die down," Marjorie suggested. "Let's order some tea."

As if by magic, a waiter arrived and offered them refreshments. Marjorie ordered a pot of tea and Rachel and Sarah requested coffees.

"What was it about the commotion your friend mentioned that you didn't want to talk about?" Rachel asked.

"She's hardly a friend, we'd only just met. If I'm honest, I didn't take to her, but I can't explain why."

"Me neither," chimed Sarah.

"Stop dodging the question, Marjorie. You're worried about something. I recognise that look."

Sarah suddenly appeared concerned. "Really? What is it, Marjorie?"

"A blast from the past, that's all. I thought I recognised someone. A person I'd rather not meet, but who might be booked onto the same holiday as us. It may not be her, of course. I only got a glimpse from the back. It was the voice I recalled: loud, brash and very northern."

"Now you're being a snob," said Sarah.

"No. I don't mean it like that. The woman I know… knew had a thick northern accent and was always extremely loud."

Rachel took her trembling hand.

"Who is she?"

"If it is who I think it is, she's Ralph's cousin, a woman called Edna, Edna Parkinton."

"I wasn't expecting you to say she was a relative," admitted Rachel. "I take it you don't get on?"

"You take it right. Ralph had a wayward uncle who married beneath him – according to Ralph, not me." Marjorie stuck her chin out at Sarah, not wishing to be accused of being a snob again. "His father disapproved of the marriage, although he would have accepted it if it weren't for other misdemeanours on his son's part. We lost track after Ralph's Uncle Peter's third marriage. Edna is the daughter of his first wife, a lounge singer called Gloria, a decent, hardworking sort, actually. We were friends with Edna for a while after Ralph and I married, and kept in touch at Christmastime with cards and the odd letter for years, but I think underneath it all, she was bitter about her father missing out on the family inheritance."

Rachel's jaw dropped. "So, how did you fall out?"

"We didn't so much fall out as lose touch by mutual consent." Marjorie didn't want to discuss the row Edna had had with Ralph, not being one to wash her dirty linen in public. "I last saw her a few years ago at her mother's funeral. We didn't have much to say to each other. Her brother, Clive – he's even more bitter than she is – kept us apart. So we haven't stayed in touch, and as she isn't a blood relative as such, I admit, I gave it up.

"I heard on the grapevine that her own husband died last year and sent her a sympathy card, but I wasn't invited to the funeral. I've been feeling guilty about her family's side of things for some time now, if I'm honest. Ralph inherited everything and Peter was written out of the will."

"It does sound harsh," Sarah said.

"Indeed it was. But, you see, Ralph's uncle, as well as being a womaniser, was also a compulsive gambler and would have brought the family name to ruin, and no doubt have gambled away the money from the business their father had worked so hard to build up."

"Was the uncle, Peter, also titled?" asked Rachel.

"No. My husband inherited the title. All Peter did was accumulate enormous debts. It wouldn't surprise me if he didn't sometimes use Ralph's title as surety. I'm afraid he wasn't honest, neither was his third wife. Edna's mother was different. As well as being hardworking, she was a woman with scruples. If anyone could have brought Peter into line, it would have been her, but he left her in poverty while pursuing other women and frequenting casinos. She divorced him in the end, but received nothing but debt in the settlement. Another reason Edna is so bitter, I expect."

"Did no-one try to help her?" Sarah asked in dismay.

"Yes, Ralph's father did, but Gloria – Edna's mother – wouldn't accept anything; she was a proud woman. He paid for Edna's wedding just before he died, the only thing her mother ever accepted from the family. Peter didn't even go to the wedding – embarrassed, I expect, at being unable to foot the bill. It was tradition in those days for the bride's father to pay."

"Perhaps it wasn't this Edna you saw, Marjorie," said Rachel.

"Well, if it is, I feel sorry for her. Sounds like she and her mother had a tough life," said Sarah.

"Don't," answered Marjorie. "She doesn't deserve pity." The names Edna had called Ralph came flooding back. Marjorie was pleased when Rachel intervened to dispel the tension.

"Come on, the queue's died down, let's go and register."

Chapter 2

The travel agent had arranged a dinner for the holiday party joining the river cruise, and Marjorie, Rachel and Sarah gathered in the hotel's Club Lounge for pre-dinner drinks to meet with other travel companions. Daisy Young, the youthful blonde woman who had been yelled at earlier, had introduced herself when registering them. She now stood at the door, ticking people off her list.

"Good evening, Lady Snellthorpe—"

"Marjorie, please."

A genuine smile lit up Daisy's youthful face and pale green eyes. "Okay, Marjorie, please help yourself to drinks and mingle as much as you like. It's not compulsory, though."

"Right person for that job," remarked Rachel as they moved past a small gathering.

"Quick! Over there," Marjorie ushered her two friends into a corner on the far side of the room.

"What's wrong?" asked Rachel.

"It's her," Marjorie hissed. "One o'clock, dressed in emerald green."

Rachel and Sarah peered over her shoulder in the direction she had indicated.

"If she's on the same cruise after all, I don't see how you can avoid her for a whole fortnight. Why don't you get it over with and make amends?" Sarah had the annoying habit of wanting to be a peacemaker. Whilst she had a point, Marjorie wasn't quite ready to succumb so easily. Not just yet.

"Oh, look! There's Greta Mitchell," Marjorie waved at the surly woman heading towards them, followed by her meek husband.

"This is the woman I was telling you about, Larry. The lonely one who witnessed the fight in reception while you were absent." The pointed dig was not lost on the small man, who sighed quietly.

Marjorie's eyes widened. Although resenting being described as lonely, she ignored that part.

"It was hardly a fight—"

"If Faith Weathers hadn't intervened, it could well have been." Greta didn't appear happy with her exaggerated version of events being challenged. Marjorie had no intention of discussing the matter further as Edna might appear at any moment and reveal their relationship.

"Is that the other guide's name? We haven't met her yet."

"Yes, she's the lead guide. To be honest, I didn't recognise her at first; she's dyed her hair black. We've met her before, haven't we, Larry?" Without giving her husband an opportunity to reply, Greta whispered to Marjorie, "I have some dirt on her. She doesn't remember me, but I remember her very well indeed."

"I thought this was your first cruise?"

"It is, that's not how we met. In fact, there are several people in this room I could tell you all about."

"Ladies!" A tall man of average build joined them. Marjorie noticed he was wearing a brown toupee, not quite matching the grey sideburns. His twinkling blue eyes and a well-trimmed mascaraed moustache added to the appearance of one not being comfortable with the ageing process. He'd appeared behind Larry and Greta as if he were an old friend, but his gaze made a beeline for Marjorie's young friends. He immediately focussed his attention on Rachel. "I feel like I've died and gone to heaven. I had no idea I'd be surrounded by such beauty."

Rachel, tall with long blonde hair and blue eyes, was stunningly beautiful, but her looks were not something she was entirely comfortable with, often drawing unwelcome attention. Marjorie knew the man's approach was nothing new; Rachel had heard it all before. She tutted. The man was old enough to be her friend's grandfather.

What is it with some older men that they think they can be attractive to young women? Marjorie mused before intervening.

"Good evening to you too, Mr?"

"Tyler, Horace Tyler—"

"Mr Tyler, I'm Marjorie. Have you met Greta and Larry Mitchell?" Marjorie shook Horace's hand, turning at the same time towards the little man, who flushed. Greta's straight face reacted angrily at the interruption of her would-be gossip. Horace Tyler let out a loud snort, clearly not happy with having his attention drawn away from Rachel, either.

"Can't say I have. How do you do?" Horace was about to turn back towards Rachel when Greta snarled at him.

"Oh, really? We've met before, all right."

The man's brow furrowed. Greta had recovered her disappointment at being unable to continue her conversation with Marjorie now she'd found new prey. She immediately commandeered the brash stranger, smiling through tight lips coated in bright-red lipstick. Unlike Daisy Young's smile, Greta's couldn't have been more false.

Horace Tyler appeared thrown for a moment and scratched his head. Rachel and Sarah seized the opportunity to move elsewhere, giving Marjorie a smile of appreciation. She followed them, hearing him introducing himself to Larry and Greta again in a slightly less self-assured tone.

"I don't believe we've met before. Perhaps you recognise me from company posters – Tyler Avionics, I'm sure you've heard of us." His confidence seemed to have returned.

"Oh dear. He's showing off about who he is and what he owns now," chuckled Marjorie when she joined her friends.

"Don't worry, Marjorie. People will soon clique off like they do on sea cruises once they settle in. We don't need to spend too much time with him, or the Mitchells, for that matter." Sarah was trying to sound reassuring, but Marjorie didn't believe the likes of Horace Tyler or Greta Mitchell would give up quite so easily. She shook her head.

"I used to have a cousin called Horace. No longer with us, I'm afraid. He was rather brash, too."

Sarah chuckled. "You'd better stay out of his way, Rachel. He's got an eye for younger women, from what I saw."

Rachel punched her friend on the arm. "He seems to be doing all right with Greta for now."

Marjorie turned to see Greta's feeble husband had been sent away to fetch drinks.

Rachel continued. "They're well suited, if you ask me! What was Greta saying about the tour leader, Faith Weathers?"

"Who knows? Implied she had some dirt on her. Idle gossip, I should imagine. And after her description of the argument earlier, I suspect whatever Greta knows, or thinks she knows, will be embellished with untruths. She also hinted at knowing things about other people in the room, too. I do hope she isn't going to cause trouble."

"I fear she will. I really don't like the way she treats her husband. It's hardly a respectful relationship, is it?" Sarah said.

"Not at all. I wonder periodically how some marriages keep going. I doubt there'll be any great Golden Wedding Anniversary celebrations."

"Maybe they're happier than they seem. They have come on a cruise, after all. On another topic, I do like the name Faith Weathers," Rachel remarked.

"Speaking of weather, the forecast for the next two weeks is excellent," said Sarah.

"I knew it wouldn't be long in a roomful of Brits before I heard someone mention the weather." A slim, friendly looking woman with a purple-rinse perm and an American accent joined them.

"We can't help ourselves," laughed Marjorie.

"Anyway, hi, I'm Jana, Jana Tipsarovic."

"What a lovely name," remarked Marjorie.

"It's Serbian, but I grew up and lived most of my life in the States. I moved over to England five years back. My husband's English."

Marjorie was introducing herself and her two companions when a man with tight-white afro hair arrived, carrying two glasses of champagne.

"Here you are," he handed Jana a glass. His accent was Oxford English.

"This is my husband, Gerald. Gerald Banks."

Gerald frowned at his wife. Marjorie's eyebrows furrowed, confused.

"Your surnames are different," she said.

"Oh, that. Yes, we get that a lot," said Jana. "We are married, honest." She crossed her heart with her right hand. "I keep my birth name for professional purposes. I'm professor of African studies in Bristol, semi-retired now, but old habits and all that. I'm actually double-barrelled, but it's so long winded to say Tipsarovic-Banks, don't you think? Gerald would rather I go by Banks now, but I cling tight to my roots."

A further round of introductions followed, with Gerald turning out to be as pleasant as his attractive wife.

"For a moment there, I thought you were as old-fashioned on the subject of surnames as I am." His dark brown eyes shone with humour as he teased Marjorie. She could tell a kindred spirit when she met one.

"Old-fashioned? I'll have you know, I'm a thoroughly modern octogenarian!" she quipped back and Gerald let out a huge guffaw. Marjorie sensed Rachel and Sarah warming to the unusual couple, too. Things were looking up following their initial encounters.

Chapter 3

Marjorie observed the tour leader, Faith Weathers, a competent-looking woman approaching fifty with a thick layer of foundation, circulating through the room, chatting happily with guests. When she approached their group, Marjorie couldn't help noticing the pretty elongated face.

"Good evening, we met earlier," she shook Jana's hand. "I'm Faith Weathers," she addressed Marjorie and the others. "I hope your rooms are comfortable and you're excited about tomorrow. If there's anything I can do to help…"

The spiel was automatic, but still came across as genuine. Jana was first to acknowledge their hostess.

"Good to meet you again, Faith. What a lovely name."

"I was saying the same," added Rachel.

Faith flashed a smile at both women in response, and Jana continued.

"Our room is just perfect, isn't it, Gerr?"

"Indeed it is," answered Gerald, taking Faith's hand and shaking it. "We were just getting to know some charming fellow passengers – apart from one, that is," he winked at Marjorie and guffawed again. The two of them had gelled almost immediately, and Marjorie suspected their wicked senses of humour would be equal to each other.

"That's good to hear, on both counts," replied Faith, having checked Marjorie had accepted the joke.

"I'm Marjorie, and these are my friends and companions, Rachel and Sarah."

After a few pleasantries about the hotel and how they were all looking forward to joining the *Amethyst River Queen* the next morning, Faith moved along to the next group.

"I like her," Jana remarked. "Sad eyes, though."

Marjorie had been thinking the same thing and was impressed with Jana's astute observational skills. Clearly an expert reader of people. Her eyes followed Faith's movements and she nudged Rachel and nodded in the tour leader's direction.

"Oh, well spotted."

"What?" quizzed Sarah, who had been distracted by Jana.

"Our hostess, Faith Weathers, has just given Greta Mitchell a wide berth. Perhaps she recognised the woman after all," Marjorie explained.

Jana and Gerald had started a conversation with another woman, so Rachel lowered her voice. "I don't blame her, judging by the short time we spent with the rather poisonous Greta. Look, she's having a heated discussion with someone else now."

They watched as Greta Mitchell's lips, as tightened as the rest of her, moved up and down.

"Oh dear. She is an unpleasant sort, isn't she?" said Marjorie, watching as Greta hissed something at a tall bleach-blonde woman wearing a bright-red thigh-length cocktail dress who looked to be around sixty.

"Where's Carry Larry?" asked Rachel.

"What makes you call him that?" Marjorie quizzed.

"Every time I've seen him so far, he's been carrying something or fetching something for his demanding wife."

Marjorie chuckled. "I do hope we can keep our distance from them. No offence, but I don't want to hear the gossip about Faith, or anyone else for that matter; I just want to enjoy a charming glide down the Rhine and the Danube."

Rachel squeezed Marjorie's hand. "Don't worry, we'll avoid the sharp-tongued Greta Mitchell, I promise."

"What long legs." Sarah was more focussed on the woman Greta appeared to be threatening. "I hope my legs are that good at her age."

"Tut, Sarah. She's a spring lamb compared to me," laughed Marjorie.

Jana interrupted their conversation to introduce the woman she and Gerald had just met. "This is Marjorie, Rachel and Sarah, and this is Florence Watson, or do we call you Flo?"

"I'll answer to either, but I prefer my given name. Some of my close friends do call me Flo." The woman held out her hand to Marjorie, who shook it.

"I'm the same. Marjorie I was born and Marjorie I will die," she chuckled.

Rachel and Sarah shook the newcomer's hand. Florence had a round, open face with large brown eyes. Her permed brown hair was highlighted with silver streaks and shone from a glitter application.

"Good to meet you," said Rachel. "Have you met many other people yet?"

Florence glanced anxiously towards Greta, who was still in a deep discussion with the bleach blonde. Marjorie didn't miss the moment.

"Not really," Florence said. "I'm meeting a friend the day after tomorrow, he's joining the holiday from Cologne."

Marjorie noticed a slight blush and brighter eyes.

"His name's Christoph."

"I hope you don't mind me asking," interrupted Sarah, "but are you Florence Watson of FW Pet Herbals?"

"Wow! I didn't know anyone would tie the two together, but yes, I am. How did you know?"

"I had a cat for many years and Mum swore by your products. Before she treated Pickles, I looked you up to check you weren't a quack. The reviews were astonishing, and he benefited from your anti-anxiety drops through many Bonfire Nights and New Year celebrations. We lost him a while back." Sarah's eyes stared at the floor and she chewed her bottom lip.

"I'm sorry to hear that. Only a pet owner can understand how painful it is to lose a member of the family. I'm a cat lover, too; I'm pleased we could be of help. I'm thinking of selling the business; actually, that's what I'm meeting Christoph about, so this is partly a work break for me."

The friendly Jana and Gerald again became engrossed in conversation with Florence, while Marjorie and the others listened in. Then Marjorie's heart sank as a woman heading their way drew her attention.

Chapter 4

"Well, if it ain't Marge Snellthorpe! Fancy seeing you here, though I should have guessed this would be your sort of thing."

Marjorie's larger-than-life cousin had finally put in her 'I'm here, world, look at me' appearance. Gerald, Jana and Florence stopped talking and turned to see who the loud new entrant was. Marjorie noticed Sarah stifling a snicker on hearing her referred to as 'Marge'. She stretched to her full height of five foot three inches, staring up at the taller and wider woman bearing down on her, and responded with poise.

"Hello, Edna, it's been a while. How are you?"

The redheaded Edna Parkinton was not so easily disarmed.

"Who are you?" she snapped at Rachel, who had moved protectively to Marjorie's side.

"This is Rachel and that's Sarah," Marjorie cast a quick look of displeasure towards Sarah who was still trying, unsuccessfully, to conceal a smirk. "They are dear friends of mine." Turning to the rest of the gawping party, she added, "And these good people are Jana, Gerald and Florence; we've just met."

"Pleased to meet yer. I'm Marge's cousin – well, cousin-in-law, if there is such a thing. Her husband was my cousin."

"We get that. I believe cousin-in-law is an informal term used to convey a relationship with a cousin's spouse. Family trees are a hobby of mine. You must tell me all about yours, I bet it's fascinating." Jana neatly deflected the shock value the brash Edna must have been hoping for. She scowled at Marjorie before addressing Jana and staring at Gerald.

"I'm sure there'll be plenty of time to talk over the next fortnight. Every family has its bad penny, don't it, Marge? Now I must find that Faith woman and make sure she's sorted out my room, otherwise me and you might need to share, Marge. I'm sure you'll 'ave one of them enormous suites. Wouldn't that be fun?"

Edna gave Marjorie a condescending pat on the head. Marjorie's hands went straight to her immaculately permed hair, checking it wasn't ruffled. Following Edna's parting remark, she replaced the pale apprehension she suspected had been on her face with a feisty glare.

"Over my dead body." Turning to Jana and the others, she stuttered, "I can only apologise for her behaviour."

"Don't apologise to us, we've got enough embarrassing relations to fill the boat we're going to be on tomorrow. There's a thought, Gerr."

Gerald grinned and took his wife's hand. "You handle them well enough. You'd miss them if they weren't around to challenge you."

Jana stroked her chin and pointed two fingers at her temple. "Psh! Yep, like the hole I just put in my head.

Gerald's brothers can be a handful. Anyway, Marjorie – or is it Marge?"

"Oh, Marjorie, please. It's never been Marge, Edna's just teasing."

"Right. Anyway, Marjorie, I'm good with her type; I'll keep her out of your hair. Besides, I bet she's fun underneath all that bluster."

Marjorie sighed. "She used to be; now, she's rather bitter, I fear, but you're welcome to try."

"Say, you won't really have to put her up, will you? That was just a joke, right?" Jana asked.

Marjorie's resolve faltered. "I sincerely hope so."

Rachel took her friend's arm. "Don't worry, Marjorie. No-one can make you put her up. In fact, I hope she hasn't got a room, then she'll go home and leave you alone."

Marjorie patted her hand. "The thing is, dear, whether I like it or not, she's family of sorts. I don't know whether I could let that happen, not even to her."

Sarah's eyebrows shot up and her jaw dropped, but the amused wrinkle remained around the eyes.

Rachel shook her head. "She'll be fine. And if it comes to it, she can share with Sarah and I'll bunk in with you. That'll wipe the smile off her face."

Sarah folded her arms as Marjorie looked at her, appealing. "No way. Not going to happen. Your cousin. Your problem."

"I'm sure she was trying to wind you up," Florence Watson chimed in. "By the way, do any of you recognise that woman over there? I'm sure I've seen her somewhere."

Glad of the distraction, Marjorie turned to see where Florence was pointing. It was the woman Greta Mitchell had been having a long conversation with; the one whose legs Sarah had commented on. On closer inspection, she had shoulder length hair and was wearing an attractive though revealing dress stressing curves in all the right places.

"Now you mention it, I have seen her before. In a magazine, I think," said Sarah.

"Got it!" announced Jana. "She's a fashion designer. We've met her before, Gerr, at your brother's bash. Gerr's brother is in the fashion business, designs women's wear. I'm wearing one of his tonight," Jana did a twirl to show off her low-cut maroon cocktail dress, jewelled around the neck and hem. "He adds a jewel or jewels to every item of clothing he designs. These are sapphires."

"It's beautiful," said Marjorie. "Your brother must be very talented."

Gerald grinned. "He is. I actually have four brothers, Jerome's the youngest." Turning to Florence, Gerald added, "Her name's Naomi Curtis, she designs wedding dresses, and Sarah's right, she's often on the front pages of bridal magazines."

"That's it! I glance through the bridal magazines on board the *Coral* when I'm having my hair done. I'm surprised you don't recognise her, Rachel. You're the one getting married next year."

"I'm also the one who avoids reading such things. I'd rather watch paint dry."

They all giggled. Marjorie felt happier again, but an unbidden cloud had gathered which she couldn't shake off once the laughter stopped.

Jana seemed to sense Marjorie's discomfort and took her arm. "Come on, guys, you've let that Edna woman get under your skin. Let's go eat."

Guests had started to leave the lounge and were heading to the main restaurant. Jana released Marjorie and took Gerald's arm. Florence excused herself to powder her nose while Rachel and Sarah took Marjorie's trembling hands. Marjorie hoped they wouldn't be seeing too much of Edna Parkinton, Greta Mitchell, or Horace Tyler. The list was becoming a long one.

Chapter 5

There was a knock at Marjorie's door just as she was thinking of preparing for bed. Imagining it would be Rachel, she opened the door wide.

"What have you forgotten?" Her smile turned to a frown as she realised her mistake. Her mouth dried up. "What are you doing here?"

"Do you mind if I come in?"

Marjorie stood aside, allowing Edna to enter. The other woman let out a low whistle.

"Gotta hand it to you, Marge, you always travel in style. Must be the inheritance my dad missed out on, eh?"

"If you've come here to bemoan your misfortunes, don't bother. I've heard it all before, mostly from your brother."

Edna headed straight to the fridge and took a small bottle of gin from the minibar.

"May I?"

Marjorie nodded. "If you wish."

"Can I get you anything, Marge?"

"I'll have a Scotch, please." The dry mouth prevented Marjorie from reminding Edna Parkinton that this was her room and she should be the one offering drinks. She sighed heavily.

"Coming right up." Edna poured them both drinks, handing Marjorie a glass before making herself at home and perching on the arm of a chair.

"Oh, do sit down," Marjorie snapped.

Edna moved from the arm to the chair itself and downed the gin and tonic she'd prepared in one gulp, shaking her head and squinting as it hit the back of her throat.

"Dutch courage," she said, fastening her eyes on Marjorie's and rubbing her hand through black hair.

I could have sworn the hair was red earlier. "Well, what is it?" Marjorie snapped.

"I could say I was here for a friendly catch up, but you wouldn't believe me."

"No, I wouldn't, so why are you here?"

"Erm. If you put it like that, I might as well get straight to the point…" but still, Edna paused.

"Which is?"

"You see, there's been a mix up with my booking. I booked and paid for this trip a few weeks ago. It was a spur-of-the-moment thing, thought it would do me good to get away from it all. Anyway, that Faith Weathers woman thought she'd be able to sort it out, but it seems their room allocation is full. She tried the cruise line, but the boat's full and no-one's pulled out. Seems there was a technical glitch in the computer system, and the room they allocated me was double-booked. Just my luck the other people checked in first."

Edna put her hand up to prevent Marjorie from saying what they both knew would come next.

"I know, I'm not going to moan, or bemoan my misfortune, as you so graciously put it, and I know you don't owe me anything, but I've been really down lately and I was so looking forward to this cruise…"

"You can't seriously be suggesting what I think you are? I thought you were joking when you mentioned sharing earlier."

"To be honest, I was. When Faith told me there was nothing she could do, I was all ready to pack my bags when I thought maybe it wasn't such a bad idea after all. It could work and I would be company for you. You must be lonely."

"I'm not lonely and I have company, thank you."

"Okay. It would be doing me a big favour. We used to get on all right, would it be such a bad thing?"

"Do you want me to answer that honestly?" Edna eyed the minibar again, but Marjorie continued, "Look, Edna, we are poles apart, it just wouldn't work. Even if I wanted to help, we'd get on each other's nerves and end up ruining both of our holidays. I'm sure the cruise line can offer you an alternative date."

"Yeah, they already did that, but this week's the first anniversary of Dennis's death, so I just wanted to be as far from Burnley as I could get. It really wouldn't be such a bad thing, I'm sure they'd give you a refund on your single supplement."

"It's not about the money, Edna. I'm sorry, I just can't help."

"You mean won't."

"If you put it that way, I'm not disposed to help."

Marjorie couldn't miss the glistening behind the steely brown eyes as Edna heaved herself from the chair.

"I guessed as much, but it was worth a try. I shouldn't have asked. Have a great cruise, Marge. It was good seeing you again."

Marjorie followed Edna to the door and watched as she walked, head held high, along the corridor. She called after her, "Wait a minute." Returning to her room, Marjorie collected the key card and left again. A minute later, she joined Edna who stood waiting in the corridor.

"If I agree to your request, there are going to be conditions."

Expectant eyes locked onto Marjorie's. "Try me."

"You will sleep on a bed settee in the sitting room. I'll ask for it to be made up."

"I can do that, no problem."

"You will not be my guest, so I expect you to do your own thing, find your own entertainment, and keep out of my way."

Edna nodded. "If that's what you want, I can agree to that okay."

"Finally, you will, under no circumstances, refer to me as Marge or any name other than Marjorie for the duration."

Edna smirked, but Marjorie couldn't be irritated as the other woman wiped tears from her eyes with a tissue and looked down at her.

"What made you change your mind?"

"The lack of histrionics and pleading helped – I can't bear such things – but at the end of the day, it was what you said about Dennis and the upcoming anniversary. I may not understand you, Edna, and we may not like each other very much, but the pain of losing a soulmate, that I do understand."

Edna wiped her eyes again as a young couple passed and entered a room nearby. "I'll let Faith know what we've planned and ask her to make arrangements. I'm sure she'll want to check with you, so I expect you'll receive a call. You won't regret this, Marge… erm, Marjorie."

Marjorie forced a smile. "Goodnight, Edna." She turned and marched back to her room. *I'm certain I will regret it. Indeed, I already am*, she thought as she opened the door and entered. After closing it, she stood with her back against it for some minutes, willing her heart to stop pounding. After recovering from the shock of what she'd agreed to, she got ready for bed, sitting at the dressing table. Her eyes glistened as she stared at her reflection in the mirror.

"You would be proud of me, Ralph, of that much I'm certain."

Chapter 6

Marjorie was awake half the night, regretting being pushed into sharing her room with Ralph's cousin. When she did sleep, her dreams were filled with a cackling Edna wagging her forefinger.

"How could you have been so gullible?"

Pleased to wake up in the morning and realise it was just a dream, Marjorie called Rachel to let her know she would breakfast in her room. With food in her stomach, her perspective returned. Thankfully, she felt calmer by the time she was dressed. Her suitcase was packed and ready. She didn't need to call for help as Rachel and Sarah appeared at her door just as she opened it, offering their assistance.

They were in the queue to check out and Marjorie's thoughts were filled with how she would manage Edna Parkinton when she heard a scream followed by a commotion at the foot of the stairs, shaking her from her reverie. A crash drew loud gasps from a group of young tourists not far away, and she swivelled around. Rachel and Sarah spun in the same direction.

"Is there a doctor in the hotel?" a man called out. Someone must have fainted, Marjorie assumed, unable to see what had happened with a crowd blocking her view.

"I'm a nurse," called Sarah, and the three of them hurried towards the gathering crowd. Sarah led the way and bent down to attend to a woman lying on the floor at the foot of the flight of stairs. Marjorie and Rachel exchanged surprised glances. It was Greta Mitchell who appeared to have taken a tumble down the stairs. The crumpled heap with startled, wide unyielding eyes told Marjorie the unfortunate woman was dead.

Sarah confirmed her notion when she shook her head after feeling for a carotid pulse. Rachel immediately slipped into police mode and began directing the crowd away from the scene as another man stepped forward.

"I'm a doctor."

Rachel let him through, then held both arms out wide. "Step back, please. Let the medics do their job." A medical student appeared and offered assistance, joining Sarah and the doctor on the ground, although everyone could see it was a hopeless situation.

The hotel manager took over, followed by an ambulance crew; someone must have called for help. A crowd of people from the cruise party gathered to one side, some complaining about the delay. Sarah stood and, still looking at the crumpled woman lying on the floor, she and the other medics spoke with the ambulance crew for a couple of minutes before they covered Greta with a blanket. Then Marjorie saw Sarah step away and retrieve Rachel before they both rejoined her.

Rachel spoke. "Was it—?"

"Greta Mitchell. Yes, it was. I don't see her husband anywhere. I wonder if anyone's told him."

Marjorie looked on in horror as they loaded the body of Greta Mitchell onto a stretcher, her head was now covered with the blanket.

"What's happening, Marge?" Edna bustled her way through the dispersing company towards them. Marjorie was still too astonished to reprimand her cousin.

"It was a woman we met yesterday. I think she must have fallen down the stairs."

"Blimey! Not a good start to our jollies, is it?" Edna quipped.

"No, it is not," Marjorie snapped. "I hope someone's spoken to her husband." She glanced around, looking for the demure man.

Rachel took her arm. "I'm sure the hotel staff or Faith will find him. There's nothing we can do about it now. Come away, Marjorie, let's check out. Sarah's looking peaky."

Marjorie glanced at Sarah, who was again speaking to the doctor who had come to her assistance. She did look pale. Nodding, she turned back and headed towards the reception desk. Edna followed, and Sarah joined them just as they reached the desk.

"Will she be all right?" Edna asked.

"I'm afraid not," said Sarah. "I think her neck was broken in the fall. No-one seems to have seen anything, according to the medical student who joined me and the doctor. The manager was shocked, said he'd been told there was a crowd at the top of the stairs, but no-one saw how she fell. The doctor said he'd been in the check-out queue and didn't see her fall. He told us he recognised her from online videos. It appears she was notorious. Her videos and blog were a modern-day gossip column. Caustic, was the term he used. His wife follows the blog; he says she finds it entertaining."

"Someone like that could have a lot of enemies," Marjorie said thoughtfully, remembering how unpleasant Greta had been last evening.

"What was 'er name?" quizzed Edna, whose Lancashire accent had slipped back into gear.

"Greta Mitchell," Sarah answered.

"Oh, now I know who you mean. She writes under the name of Pru Avenger. Her blog and video channel are called *The Pruning Fork* – rather clever, I always thought."

Marjorie noticed Rachel's eyes scrunch as they were apt to do when she was thinking. She looked up at her cousin-in-law.

"How do you know all this?"

"I follow the blog, though I'm not a fan of the video channel, too *Jeremy Kyle* for my liking. The blog is well written, despite the fact it spews sheer vitriol. It spills out a lot of hatred, but because she uses canny language, the worst is somehow disguised. I pity the poor people she puts under her pruning fork; she didn't pull her punches. Frightening, but at the same time, it is – or, should I say, was – witty."

"I can't see how anyone could be interested in reading such garbage." Marjorie stiffened. "And as for finding the public humiliation of others funny, well, I will never understand such things."

"All right, keep yer 'air on, Marge. I expect most of it was exaggerated anyway," Edna retorted.

Marjorie remembered how Greta had exaggerated the argument at reception, and then how the woman had implied she knew things about Faith Weathers and others in the travel party.

"Oh dear, I've just had a terrible thought about this."

"Me too," agreed Rachel.

Sarah's face reddened. "Oh no. Not again, you two. Don't start. It was just a tragic accident, don't bring any of your murder theories on my river escape."

"What murder theories?" asked Edna.

"Didn't you know? These two sleuths can't seem to avoid murder. Killers just wait for them to be present before they strike, all too frequently."

Sarah's voice had risen by several octaves, but the sarcasm in her tone couldn't disguise the fact that what she said was true. Edna's loosening eyelashes momentarily mesmerised Marjorie as they flickered unsteadily from side to side. Edna was clearly trying to process what she was hearing.

"It's true. Rachel is a detective and murder seems to follow her around," Marjorie said triumphantly, pleased at Edna being rendered speechless for once.

Rachel grinned. "Don't you blame me, it's not as if I bring these people with me. And you're as much a murder magnet as I am, Lady Marjorie Snellthorpe."

"Can I just point out before you start again," Sarah cut in, "that the woman fell down the stairs. An accident. End of…"

Edna straightened the blonde wig that had slipped to one side before finding her voice. "Yeah, I agree with her. I don't like the idea of being on holiday with a murderer."

"But can either of you be certain?" Although she felt slightly guilty at making light of a woman's death, Marjorie was beginning to enjoy herself.

Chapter 7

The cruise party finally gathered together in the lobby after checking out. Faith appeared well made up and fresh as she welcomed them, considering what had just happened. Soon, their suitcases were being loaded on to the waiting coach and they were shepherded from the hotel to board.

Daisy Young, who was waiting outside, spoke to each person as she ticked passenger names off her list. Faith moved to the coach entrance ready to answer questions and assist anyone needing help with the steps. The coach driver and bell boys from the hotel were busy loading suitcases into the luggage compartment at the side.

"Well organised," said Sarah. Rachel agreed with her friend, then bent down to whisper to Marjorie.

"Are you okay?"

"Yes, I—"

"Marge!" Marjorie heard the loud voice before Edna put in her appearance, hurtling towards them past the orderly queue like a steam train, much to the disgust of other passengers. Marjorie observed the wide-eyed dress designer, Naomi Curtis, muttering to a few people around her.

Rachel's jaw dropped as Edna arrived, and her body language told Marjorie she was ready to fight her corner. Amidst all the excitement of what had happened before their departure, Marjorie hadn't found the opportunity to tell her young friends about her agreement with her cousin-in-law, who had raced off to fetch her suitcase after their earlier conversation.

"It's all right, dear." Marjorie placed a hand on Rachel's arm before turning around to address Edna. "We talked about this," she hissed.

"What? Oh, that… all right, Marjorie it is, then. Good morning to you. What a lovely day, I can't wait for our new adventure, can you?"

Before Marjorie could say anything else, Edna barged to the front of the queue, after giving her name to Daisy – as if she had to. Marjorie felt sure it was ingrained in the poor young woman's brain. Rachel gave the rest of their names and a bemused Sarah turned to Marjorie as they watched Edna sweep past Faith on to the coach.

"She managed to get a room then? Pity."

Marjorie's heart was in her stomach, her dry mouth unable to get any words out. She headed silently towards Faith. Rachel and Sarah's concern for her was palpable.

"Lady Snellthorpe," said Faith. "Good morning. I trust you're well?"

"Please call me Marjorie," she felt the words come out automatically, but they sounded hollow.

"Well, Marjorie, it's a very generous thing you're doing. I hope your cousin appreciates it." Faith's sympathetic eyes almost caused Marjorie to crack.

"You can't be doing what I think you're doing," Rachel whispered as a hotel employee helped Marjorie up the step on to the coach.

"I, erm…"

"Up here, Marge! Sorry… Marjorie. I've saved you a seat." The loud voice boomed from the back end of the coach, causing those already aboard to turn their heads, some amused, some disapproving.

"We don't have to sit with her as well, do we?" Sarah rolled her eyes.

Marjorie's courage returned as she straightened. "Don't worry, dear, I'll handle her." Holding her cousin's eyes, Marjorie took a place next to an elderly gentleman sitting alone. She hadn't realised before she sat down that the man was Horace Tyler. She sighed. *Could this day get any worse?*

Rachel grinned at Marjorie, clearly pleased she wasn't the one sitting next to Horace. Then she and Sarah took the seats behind them.

"Good morning. I hope I'm not intruding," Marjorie said, realising she hadn't asked if the seat was taken in her hurry to snub Edna.

"Not at all. We met last night, I believe." Horace turned his head to smile at Rachel and Sarah.

"So we did. I think I heard you say you're in avionics?"

That did the trick; Marjorie was treated to a lesson on avionic history, or more accurately, on how Horace Tyler had changed the world. Some of the information was interesting, but Horace's penchant for self-aggrandisement was off-putting. Still, it was better than sitting next to Edna, Marjorie consoled herself as she half listened to Horace on their journey to where their ship would be docked.

Marjorie was tuning in to Rachel and Sarah chatting happily behind her when a thought came to her. She waited for Horace Tyler to pause for a breath before speaking.

"Do you know anyone else on the cruise?"

"Not yet, but I hope to get to know a few people." He turned hopefully to peek back at Rachel, but she was engrossed in conversation with her best friend. His eyes returned to Marjorie. "Why do you ask?"

"No reason, but I thought I heard Mrs Mitchell say she knew you after I introduced the two of you last night."

Horace stiffened, a cloud forming over his features, which Marjorie had to admit were not bad looking. He obviously kept himself in trim.

"She said she did; I don't remember her, though. Some women like to use that line with me, especially when they realise I'm well off."

"Did you hear about the accident?"

"Couldn't help but hear about it. It's all people have been talking about, and why we've been delayed two hours before leaving. There'd better be a drink in this to make up for the inconvenience."

"I hardly feel a woman's death should be referred to as an inconvenience," Marjorie snapped.

"Quite. It wasn't that I was referring to, tragic as it was, although we all have to go sometime, don't we?"

Marjorie detected a hint of celebration in his tone. "Are you certain you didn't know her?"

"Never seen her before, and though I don't like to speak ill of the dead, I think the cruise will be better without her. Seemed a nasty sort, if you know what I mean." Horace looked out of the window, a wide grin reflecting in the glass.

Odd, thought Marjorie. *I could have sworn from his reaction last evening that he had recognised Greta.* Mind you, having spent a short amount of time in her presence, she couldn't blame him for not wanting to associate himself with the woman. She couldn't shake the feeling that Greta Mitchell had made many enemies along the line. Faith had clearly gone out of her way to avoid her, and now Horace Tyler was denying knowing her while he appeared to be triumphant about her death. Then there was the wedding dress designer, Naomi Curtis, who clearly hadn't been enjoying the conversation with Greta that Marjorie had witnessed the night before.

Was the tragic death of Greta Mitchell serendipity or the opposite? A conviction there was more to it than an unfortunate accident settled itself on Marjorie as she observed the gleeful Horace Tyler staring out of the window, humming.

Chapter 8

The *Amethyst River Queen*, although much smaller than a cruise ship, stood 180 metres in length and comprised four decks. As soon as the guests stepped off the coach, a welcome party consisting of the captain and ship's officers lined the boarding ramp to greet them.

"Now you wouldn't get this on the *Coral Queen*," Marjorie teased Sarah.

"I don't get any welcome at all, remember. I have to board by the crew entrance, but I'm so looking forward to this," Sarah countered.

"Me too," said Rachel. "And I always receive a very warm welcome on the *Coral Queen*. Granted, it doesn't usually include the captain. I've always wanted to visit Budapest."

"Well, you've chosen a slow way of getting there," Sarah laughed.

"It will make the arrival all the more pleasing, dear," said Marjorie.

Faith was speaking to a handsome young man in his forties with short fair hair when they approached the line-up.

"Welcome to Queen River Cruises, ladies," he said. "I'm Gustav, official tour guide attached to your party. I'll be assisting Faith and Daisy with local knowledge. If there's anything you need to know, please ask. I know the Rhine and the Danube like – how do you say? Like the back of my hand?"

Marjorie detected a Dutch twang, but couldn't be certain. "Thank you, we will. I'm Marjorie and these are my friends, Rachel and Sarah."

Gustav's eyes lit up at the sight of Rachel and Sarah, both beautiful in their own way. They were not only beautiful on the outside, they were gold dust on the inside, which is what made Marjorie proud to be with them; she would never have to apologise for their behaviour. She sighed, suspecting the next fortnight would be taken up with apologising for someone else's behaviour.

They continued their way along the line as each officer introduced themselves. Marjorie couldn't help noticing Horace and the attractive fashion designer, Naomi, two people ahead. Horace was slowing down proceedings by taking up more time with the captain than was polite.

"And I can assure you, Captain, you, your officers and your ship could benefit from some of the things we have to offer at Tyler Avionics."

The flicker of a frown crossed Faith's face, but she quickly recovered before calling out, "Move along, please. There will be plenty of opportunity to chat to the ship's crew over the next two weeks."

The captain threw Horace an apologetic glance, shrugging his shoulders before hurriedly turning to the next passenger behind him. Horace flashed a glare at Faith, which was ignored as the friendly guide was now welcoming the next few passengers. The spurned man let out a loud "Harrumph" and moved on.

"He also writes a blog!" Sarah whispered to Marjorie while the ship's chef, who was next in line, welcomed Rachel.

"What is it with this modern-day trend to share diaries with the world?" Marjorie replied. "Surely that's all these things are? And I dread to think what sort of a blog that man would write. He's a narcissist if ever I saw one."

Sarah pulled out her phone. "What was the surname again?"

"Sarah, put that away," Marjorie chastised. Sarah giggled and did as she was asked.

"You fell for that."

Following brief introductions to the majority of the ship's crew, Marjorie was relieved to step aboard the vessel. Rachel opened the brochure pack they had been given before leaving the hotel.

"We're on deck three, but as they're still loading the suitcases, shall we find one of the sun lounges? I could do with a coffee."

Marjorie glanced to her left, noticing another gangway leading to the dockside where suitcases packed on metal trolleys were being carefully loaded on to the ship.

"I wouldn't say no to a cup of tea. Quick, let's move." She heard Edna's voice getting closer, but was relieved, following an anxious glance backwards, to see her roommate was being held up.

"It's all right, that's your new boyfriend Horace Tyler blocking her path." Rachel did a good takeoff of the flirtatious man's accent. "He's probably waiting to catch another word with the captain."

"Or to give Faith a flea in her ear for stopping him boring the man to death," said Sarah.

"And don't you be ridiculous, Rachel, he's not my new anything. You should know better. Besides, it was you he was flirting with last night, and he's too young for me. Not that I would be interested even if he wasn't." Marjorie chuckled. "What's more, I'm convinced he knew Greta Mitchell, you know."

"I wondered about that. I heard you quizzing him on the bus," replied Rachel.

"I don't know about you, but I'd still rather we hurry; we don't want your cousin to catch up with us," said Sarah, taking Marjorie's arm. "Lead the way, Rachel. You're the one with the ship's map."

"Cousin-in-law, dear, cousin-in-law. I don't have such relatives."

"We all have such relatives," laughed Sarah.

"You must tell me who you're referring to."

"Hopefully, you'll never meet him. Although he does live in London somewhere."

"I don't know if you've heard, my dear, but London is a big place," Marjorie teased.

They found a beautiful wide-open sun lounge on deck four with plenty of tables and parasols for the sixty-four guests Faith had said would be on board, thirty-two of whom, including Faith and Daisy, were in their travel party.

"Probably only thirty now," Marjorie said.

"Pardon?" quizzed Rachel.

"Oh, nothing. I was just thinking out loud."

They found a table and nodded to a few other guests who had obviously shared the same idea to avoid any rush at reception. No sooner had their hot drinks arrived than the moment Marjorie had dreaded dampened her pleasure.

"There you are! I've been looking all over for you."

More like you followed us straight from boarding, Marjorie thought. Why was it she found this woman so irritating?

"Are you and your young friends settling in all right?"

Marjorie glared at the woman. The conditions she had laid before Edna the previous evening seemed to have completely slipped her mind. Deliberately, no doubt. She didn't trust herself to speak.

Sarah intervened. "We are, thank you. I take it you didn't get the problems with your booking sorted?"

"A right mess they made of that! All settled now, though. Marge… er, Marjorie's come to the rescue. I'm bunking in with her."

"So we gathered," said Rachel. "That's really kind of you, Marjorie."

Marjorie forced a smile. "I suppose it is. But it shouldn't interfere with our holiday. Edna assured me she will do her own thing and leave us alone," she said pointedly. "Rachel's getting married next year and this is a special treat; I'm sure you understand."

"Congratulations," Edna's tone was flat. "Well, I'll be off, then. Don't worry, I won't get in your way." Edna stretched her short neck to raise her head before fluttering reapplied false eyelashes at a young waiter and taking a seat at a table nearby. "Young man, could you get me a cappuccino?"

"Now I feel mean. She's doing this deliberately." Marjorie stared at her cousin's back.

"What made you agree to let her share with you in the first place?" Rachel asked.

"I suppose it is time to explain how it came about. She arrived at my room last night after Faith broke it to her there had been a mix up with her booking. Faith couldn't find her a room, despite trying every option open to her. I suggested to Edna that she should accept the cruise line's offer of a future date, but," Marjorie lowered her voice just in case Edna could hear, "she gave me a bit of a sob story about it being the first anniversary of her husband Dennis's death this coming week. I suppose it pulled at my heartstrings. I remembered the first year after losing Ralph. It was such a hard time. The pain never goes away, you know, but it gets easier."

Rachel took her hand and squeezed it.

Marjorie recovered herself, straightening up. "I capitulated after refusing at first, but insisted that if I allow her to share my room, she must leave us alone, and refer to me as Marjorie, not Marge. Neither of which seems to be going well thus far."

Sarah chuckled. "I don't see how anyone could call you Marge. You're definitely a Marjorie." Lowering her voice to match Marjorie's, she continued. "Is it my imagination, or was she a redhead last night?"

"She was. Definitely wears wigs," answered Rachel.

Marjorie giggled. "Yes, it was a black one when she came to my room last night."

"And now it's grown six inches and gone blonde." Sarah laughed. "I assume the eyelashes are false as well? She certainly stands out in a crowd."

Marjorie shook her head. "Precisely, she always wore a lot of makeup, and I do believe her hair was brown before she went grey. At least she hasn't lost her flair where that's concerned."

"I think she looks good for her age," said Sarah. "I love her clothes."

Marjorie agreed. When it came to dressing on a budget, Edna had always been able to carry it off.

"I would imagine she inherited her dress sense from her mother, although it can be a little too loud for my taste."

"Right, that's enough about your cousin-in-law. Come on, Marjorie, let's finish our drinks, check in and go find our rooms," Rachel suggested.

Chapter 9

Edna stared out around the sunroom, noticing nothing in particular, picking up her cappuccino at regular intervals and enjoying the flavour. Why did Marjorie have to be such a snob? Yes, she had to agree it was good of her cousin-in-law to let her share her room, albeit reluctantly, but she could be a bit more gracious about it. It wasn't as if Edna wanted to share, either. The muddle with her room was just a part of the run of bad luck she had experienced of late. Her dad would have maintained that fortune was bound to turn in her favour eventually, but it never had for him. He could have had so much, and in turn, she wouldn't have had to watch her mother struggle to make ends meet when she and her brother, Clive, were young.

Gloria Snellthorpe had sensibly divorced Edna's dad before he ruined his and their lives even more, but she hadn't had a bitter bone in her body and never spoke a word against the man. Perhaps that was why Clive was so bitter; he didn't know the half of it, being the younger sibling. Even if their dad had inherited a chunk of money, and by some miracle managed to use it sensibly, she doubted she and Clive would have got much because of his subsequent marriages and her mother's constant refusal to accept any help that her grandfather offered. She hadn't realised growing up how much the Snellthorpe grandparents had wanted to be involved in their lives, but her mother eventually told her not to hate them for what they did to her father. Just before she died, she revealed all.

"Don't be bitter, Edna. They were good people. Your dad was a rotten apple, that's all. Trust me, they tried to help him and us."

It was hard for Edna to hear stuff like that when she'd hated the Snellthorpe family most of her adult life. Even now, she fought with her feelings about what her mother had revealed. When she was at her worst, particularly when she was with Clive, she revelled in going over the same old ground about their misfortunes.

Edna stared into space, realising it was only when she was with Clive that she felt so much anger. He'd inherited the gambling gene – if there was such a thing – from their dad. She herself had married a good man and actually led a happy life. It was just that nagging doubt Clive sewed that their mother had made it all up about her grandparents wanting to help to keep the peace.

As she remembered the warmth of her mother's smile and her soothing voice, Edna felt a tear spring from nowhere. She wondered if Marjorie felt guilty about Ralph Snellthorpe inheriting everything from his father after he had written her dad out of the will; perhaps that's why she was so rude.

"Hello again. Do you mind if I join you? My husband seems to have gone missing." The cheerful woman who had been so friendly the night before flashed a toothy smile. Edna appreciated the offer, along with the purple rinse.

I should have been a hairdresser, she mused, pulling herself from her ruminations and grinning back.

"Please do."

"Thank you. I wasn't sure whether to disturb you. You seemed so deep in thought."

"Not happy thoughts, I'm afraid, so the interruption is welcome. You haven't really lost your husband?"

"No. He's gone to check us in and get the key to our room. He knows I hate queuing, so he sent me off to explore."

"He's English, isn't he? I thought I heard a posh accent last night."

"Well deduced, detective. He is. I was telling your cousin yesterday, I'm not English, as you can tell; I'm Serbian, but was raised in America."

"I wouldn't have guessed the Serbia bit," Edna said honestly.

"I learned American English very early on, and I come from the paler side of the family. I could pass as a full-blooded Yankee, but I'm proud of my heritage. Gerald's ancestors were African. That's how we met: I was in Oxford as part of my job – I was a professor of African studies at Harvard, Massachusetts, and got to travel a lot. I only work part-time now, in Bristol."

"Is your husband a professor as well, then?"

"Goodness, no. I met Gerr in an African restaurant of all places. He was, and still is, in my opinion, handsome and charming. For years, we navigated a transatlantic relationship until he persuaded me to marry him and move to England. We bought a wonderful home on the outskirts of Bristol. There you have it. That's my life story in a nutshell. What about you?"

"I'd be happy to tell you about it sometime, but not just yet. I think I'd better check in before my well-to-do cousin-in-law locks me out of our room."

A glint in Jana's emerald-green eyes and the upturned crow's feet surrounding them caused Edna to burst out laughing.

"Oh, you're sharing with Marjorie, are you? I got the impression you were travelling alone."

"Not any longer. Lady Marjorie Snellthorpe's stuck with me for the next two weeks. The cruise line or travel agent overbooked my room, so Marge has come up trumps."

"A lady? I wasn't aware. Now that's going to be an interesting match. And one Gerald and me will watch closely."

Edna cackled as she headed towards the stairs leading down to reception.

***

The ship was magnificently decorated and immaculate in cleanliness. Polished veneer banisters flanked the stairs, and shiny brass-mounted wall lights exuded elegance and extravagance as only Queen Cruises could.

Marjorie had sailed with the cruise line for years, first with her husband, and more recently with Rachel. This was her first journey on a river cruise ship, though, and something she had recently added to her bucket list. She wanted to sail as many rivers of the world as she could, deciding the leisurely pace and smaller environment might suit her as she got older.

She had come to terms with the idea of finding another travelling companion to fulfil this dream with, as Rachel was soon to wed. Plus, there were only so many times her young friend could take holidays from her day job as a detective. There would be even less opportunity for Rachel to accompany her once she and her fiancé, Carlos, married. Carlos had kindly agreed that he would not object to Rachel joining her on cruises after they were married, but she would never take advantage of his or her friend's generosity.

She sighed, wondering again whether her housekeeper, Mrs Ratton, might be the ideal candidate, but she had a family of her own to tend to. If it had been Ralph who'd survived her, he would no doubt have taken Johnson, their chauffeur, as they often travelled together on fishing trips. Johnson, she knew, would gladly oblige if she asked him to accompany her, but it would be more of an endurance than a treat as he liked the simple things in life. It was a shame Edna was such a difficult woman. Now she was in a similar position to Marjorie, she would be the ideal candidate. If only they got on.

Marjorie shook the thought from her head. "Absolutely not," she muttered under her breath. Edna Parkinton was the last person on earth she would want to spend any more time with than necessary, as this fortnight would undoubtedly prove.

Chapter 10

"I have to say, you travel in style, Marjorie Snellthorpe. This room is spectacular." Edna was bursting through the expansive space, from lounge to bathroom, to bedroom, and back again like a hurricane. Marjorie felt dizzy watching, and when her over-excited guest finally returned to the sitting room, she managed to get in a word.

"When I confirmed with Faith last evening that you would be staying with me, she assured me they would make the sofa bed up each evening for you to sleep in." Marjorie nodded to the lengthy sofa in the large sitting area, hoping Edna didn't snore, but the way this cruise was going, she imagined her cousin would do just that.

The ship had eventually set sail four hours later than planned. The Dutch police had come on board to question a few passengers and crew that might have seen the accident back at the hotel. Rachel had tagged along with Sarah when she was called to give her account of events and had managed to glean some information from other passengers and a young police officer. They confirmed what Sarah had been told: that there were a number of people at the top of the stairs, mostly those joining the river cruise, when Greta seemingly stumbled and fell. The police wouldn't say who the other passengers were, but they didn't believe there was anything suspicious about the death and

– according to Rachel – their questions were perfunctory at best, giving the impression they couldn't wait to get back to the station and close the case.

A fellow passenger Rachel had spoken to said there had been quite a crowd milling around at the top of the stairs and she hoped no-one had bumped into the dead woman, causing her to fall. The passenger couldn't remember who any of the people present were as she hadn't taken much notice because she had to assist her husband, who relied on a walking stick, to make sure he didn't fall.

One thing the police told Sarah was that the dead woman's husband had been informed of the tragedy. Pitiful Larry Mitchell – not the sort of getaway anniversary he had planned, and now no getaway at all as he was most likely dealing with things in Amsterdam. Marjorie stopped for a moment, trying to recall something Greta had said when they were waiting in the hotel. What was it now?

"Blasted memory, why won't you work when I need you to?"

"Did you say something?" Edna called from the balcony where she was now exploring.

"No. Nothing." Marjorie moved through to the bedroom and found her suitcase placed on top of a luggage cover at the foot of the bed. Edna appeared behind her, dragging her two-wheeled suitcase into Marjorie's bedroom.

"Do you mind if I use some of your wardrobe space?"

Marjorie sighed; she hadn't factored in where her unwelcome guest's belongings would go.

"Of course. Use that side." She nodded to the right. "You can also use the drawers in the second chest. I won't be needing both."

The bedroom was generously apportioned, and it wasn't that Marjorie was reluctant to share the furniture; it was the thought of Edna meandering in and out of her bedroom whenever she liked that filled her with dread.

"Thanks, Marge… Marjorie."

Edna appeared happier than she had done earlier, although the incessant desire to shorten Marjorie's name was irritating. It was almost certainly deliberate. Ignoring the bait, Marjorie watched Edna remove the blonde wig, stifling an exclamation at the sight.

"How many of those do you have?" She recovered quickly, but not before feeling her mouth drop open as all that remained on top of Edna's all-but bald head were a few wisps of hair.

"About twenty in all, but I've only brought half a dozen for this trip." She hugged the mound of hair. "They're so soft and no need for hair dye, not that I have that option nowadays. I take my pick, depending on the mood. This one's my favourite." Edna put aside the blonde wig she had been hugging and picked up the bright-red shoulder-length bobbed one she had been wearing most of yesterday.

"What happened to your hair?" asked Marjorie.

"Life happened. Alopecia, they call it. I'd just finished chemotherapy for a damned cancer when – out of the blue – Dennis decided to kick the bucket. The hair's never grown back. Staff at the hospital think it was the shock of losing him, although apparently it happens sometimes.

They still think it might grow back again one day, although sometimes I think they're just saying that to humour me. In the meantime, I've got used to it, and these babies keep me company. As Dennis left me with no hair, I spent his life insurance replacing it."

Edna continued unpacking her wigs, holding each one up like a prized possession before placing them carefully in a top drawer. She finally pulled out a folded contraption that turned out to be a model head on which she placed the favourite red wig.

"I like the variety, but I do admire your snow-white locks. Your hair's always been your crowning glory, despite your height."

Marjorie ignored the barb aimed at her small stature, especially after noting her cousin's watery eyes.

"I'm sorry. I didn't know."

"Why would you? We hardly saw each other." Edna blinked away tears that threatened to spill. "I can't remember what it was we argued about now. Something over nothing, I expect."

Money, it was always money, thought Marjorie, but answered, "I expect it was." It hadn't been Marjorie Edna had rowed with, either; it had been her husband, Ralph. Marjorie once more shut that argument and his cousin's harsh words out of her head. "Has the cancer gone?"

"I had my annual check last month, and so far, so good. There's no guarantee it won't come back at some stage, but we've all got to die of something, right? Dennis and I had planned to travel the world after my treatment finished, but as I said, he went and died on me. I haven't been able to face travelling alone…"

"Until now," Marjorie finished for her.

"Yeah, until now. With the anniversary coming up, I figured, to hell with it. I'm eighty and a cancer survivor – so far; I might as well get on and do some of the things we'd planned to do together. Besides the life insurance, he left me a decent sum of money to get by on."

Edna stopped unpacking and stared out of the window as the ship moved slowly along the Rhine.

"He must have been squirrelling it away as a surprise. I never knew how much there was until I was going through papers after his death. As you know, we never had kids of our own, although we tried for years."

Marjorie realised she didn't know her cousin-in-law at all and couldn't help feeling a sadness about it. "You always said you didn't want children in your letters." *Until you stopped writing*, remained unsaid.

"We say all sorts of things when we're hurting, don't we, Marjorie?"

"I suppose we do."

Using the dressing-table mirror, Edna removed the false eyelashes she had been wearing and picked up a large toiletry bag.

"Anyway, I think I'll take a shower before changing for dinner, if you don't mind me going first?"

"Not at all." Marjorie finished her own unpacking while Edna was in the shower, mulling over what she had divulged. Usually, her cousin-in-law was the blunt 'speak before you think' kind of person. Was that side of her a coverup for what was going on underneath? Marjorie had discovered more about Edna Parkinton in the past thirty minutes than she had in decades of casual gatherings and meaningless letters. Was it the intimate surroundings of the bedroom that caused Edna to lay herself bare, or the fact she had faced death and come out on top?

Chapter 11

Mouth-watering aromas permeated the dining room, engaging Marjorie's senses as she arrived.

Edna had kept to their agreement and left the room before Marjorie emerged from her own shower. She found herself scanning the room for a glimpse of her, wondering if they could become friends. That fantasy was soon shattered as she spied the bright red wig and heard Edna's raucous laugh. She was sitting with Naomi Curtis and Horace Tyler; the latter appearing to be enjoying the attention of two women.

"Good evening, ladies. A table for three, or are you happy to share?"

"Jana and Gerald are over there waving, shall we join them?" Rachel suggested.

"Is that possible?" Marjorie strained her neck to look up at the maître d', reminded once again of her diminutive height.

"Yes, of course. Come this way."

"Blimey! He's a giant," whispered Sarah.

"I thought it was me being so tiny," chuckled Marjorie.

"No. He's got to be almost seven foot. He makes Rachel look pocket-sized, so the rest of us don't stand a chance."

Feeling better about herself by the time they reached the round table, Marjorie sat next to Jana, while Rachel sat at her side and Sarah, on Rachel's right, was next to Gerald.

"I hope we're not intruding?" she said.

"Not at all. We love company, don't we, Gerr?"

"We do indeed," Gerald beamed at Marjorie.

"Have you ordered?" Marjorie asked.

"No, we're torn, so much delicious food to choose from. I think I'm going to try the smoked sausage and Stamppot. I know the Dutch aren't renowned for their cuisine, but I believe the Rookworst sausage and Stamppot are traditional dishes."

"Indeed they are, madam." Another lanky waiter appeared behind Jana. "And delicious, I must say. Our chef Sven specialises in European food, I'm certain you'll enjoy his nightly selections."

"All right, Lucas, you've got me convinced. I'll have that."

"Any starter, madam?"

"No thanks, I'll save myself for dessert."

"And for you, sir?"

"I'll have the same, but with a shrimp cocktail starter."

Lucas introduced himself to Marjorie, Rachel and Sarah, smiling at them as he moved around the table. Once they had all ordered, they poured themselves wine from the bottles on the table that were included with the meal.

"You didn't tell me we would have a butler," said Sarah once the waiter was out of earshot.

"Don't worry, dear, it's not especially for you. Every room has butler service, but it's rather similar to stateroom service on a cruise ship," Marjorie quipped. Glancing at Rachel, she saw her friend's eyes widen, her attention drawn elsewhere.

"What is it?" Sarah asked.

"It's Larry Mitchell, I'm surprised to see him on board. I didn't think for one moment he'd carry on with his holiday."

"Surely not?" Marjorie followed Rachel's gaze, imagining her friend must be mistaken. "Goodness me, so it is; how extraordinary."

"Who's Larry Mitchell?" quizzed Jana.

"He's the husband of the woman who died tragically back at the hotel, the reason they delayed us."

"I know who you mean now. She took a tumble down the stairs, didn't she?" Jana exchanged a worried glance with her husband.

"Yes, Sarah was one of the first on the scene. Sarah's a nurse, you see, but there was nothing to be done, the poor woman was already dead. Died on impact."

"Weird her husband's here, though," Gerald agreed.

"I've been meaning to ask you, Gerald. Did you know the woman who died?" said Marjorie.

Jana's attention returned to her husband.

"What makes you ask?"

So you did know her, thought Marjorie. "I thought I saw you talking to her last night."

"Was that the woman I saw you talking to when I went for a refill?" asked Jana. "She was the one we stood behind for ages waiting to get our cocktails while she remonstrated with the waiter about not enough ice. I almost gave her a prod."

"Oh, her! No, we'd never met before, but she was chatting to many people. Naomi introduced us – remember, it was the woman Naomi was chatting to when you pointed her out last night? I think she only did it to get away from the woman. She was a bit of a chatterbox, seemed to like to be the centre of attention. Just being friendly, I think. Awful about the accident, though."

Gerald's lack of eye contact and constant touching of his nose were telltale signs he was not being truthful. Marjorie felt the nudge from Rachel's leg under the table, informing her that she too felt he was lying.

"Did either of you see what happened?" asked Marjorie.

"She tripped and fell. There was a crowd of people congregated at the top of the stairs, halted by a bottleneck caused by a rowdy young party who decided to stop and chat, so we were all making our way around them. I think her husband was there somewhere – I remember him now you've pointed him out, so I'm sure it was him – as was Faith. I think Daisy may have been up there, too, along with Naomi and the woman we were talking to last night, the one who's in pet supplies."

"Florence. Isn't that who's sitting with the dead woman's husband?" Jana said.

"Yes, that's the one sensitive soul. Anyway, I was a few feet away from Greta, and the next thing I knew, she's hurtling down the stairs, headfirst." Gerald took out a handkerchief and wiped his forehead. "Everything's a blur after that. Someone might have screamed, and a crowd raced to the bottom to help. That's when I came to find you, Jana."

"I didn't realise you were so close to it, Gerr, you didn't mention it."

"Did the police interview you? They were trying to speak to anyone in the vicinity." Rachel's laser-like gaze fixed itself on Gerald.

"No, they didn't. Not that I could have told them any more than I've just said. I heard they concluded it was a fall."

Did you indeed? thought Marjorie. *And where did you hear that?*

Rachel read her mind. "Who told you that? I was questioned and they didn't tell me what they were thinking," she persisted, being a little economical with the truth, much to Marjorie's approval.

"I think it was the pet woman, Florence, who might have said... I can't be certain... we've spoken to so many people and it has been, unsurprisingly, the topic of conversation," Gerald stammered, fiddling with his tie.

"Gerr, it must have been terrible for you. You should have said, baby." Looking at Marjorie, Jana explained, "Gerald hates anything like that ever since..."

"Ever since what?" Rachel pressed.

"It brought back horrible memories," Gerald continued. "My secretary fell down the stairs in a similarly tragic accident. It was a long time ago, but the shock never leaves you."

"Oh dear. What happened?" pressed Marjorie.

"We'd been working late. She was one of those women who always wore six-inch heels – lethal things, if you ask me. Anyway, I was still working in my office when she said goodnight. Minutes later, I heard a scream and rushed out, thinking perhaps there was an intruder."

Gerald paused for a moment.

"I found her lying there, at the bottom of the stairs," his eyes darted towards his wife. "Anyway, there was nothing I could do. The police said she must have caught her heel in the turn-up of her trousers – tailored turn-ups were not in fashion, but she loved them and looked good in them. They found a rip on the inside left turn-up where her heel must have gone through. We had steep stairs with a marble floor in reception."

Marjorie pondered whether the late-night liaison was more than work as Gerald continued to fiddle with his tie.

"It was an awful time for Gerald. I was in the States when he called me that night – or afternoon, where I was." A puzzled expression crossed Jana's face, but she said nothing else.

"Well, if you guys don't mind, I think it's time to change the subject and eat," huffed Sarah. "I'm sure Gerald and Jana have had enough of this conversation, and I don't want to be reliving the horrible experience over dinner. I'm sorry Mrs Mitchell's accident brought back such awful memories for you, though," she added with a sympathetic look towards Gerald.

"Thank you, but it was a long time ago. You're quite right, it must have been hard for you this morning. Time to move on to lighter things. Here's the food."

As they served starters, Marjorie couldn't dismiss the suspicion that the two deaths might not have been accidents. Could the charismatic Gerald Banks be a murderer? And why was Larry Mitchell behaving as if nothing had happened?

Chapter 12

After dinner, there was live entertainment: a sultry jazz singer delivered a selection of jazz and blues songs. Jana and Gerald left early and went to bed at Jana's insistence because, she explained, Gerald was still reeling from flashbacks to his secretary's accident.

As soon as they left, Rachel asked what had been on Marjorie's mind. "Do you think there was more to the relationship between Gerald and his secretary?"

"Considering his reaction, the thought had crossed my mind," said Marjorie. "Wife – or was she girlfriend back then? – away; attractive young secretary nearby."

"How do you know his secretary was attractive?" challenged Sarah. "She could have been older or younger than him and married, for all you know. Not all secretaries have affairs with their bosses, like not all nurses have affairs with doctors."

"I admit, I don't know. But I bet she was. It might be worth delving a little deeper. Anyway, it raises the question, doesn't it?" Marjorie countered.

"What question?" Sarah quizzed. "Oh no, don't tell me – it might not have been an accident at all, and the likeable Gerald Banks is now a serial killer!"

"Strictly speaking, he wouldn't be a serial killer unless there were three or more murders," Rachel said with a smirk.

Sarah inhaled a deep breath. "You two won't be satisfied unless you have a murder to investigate, will you? I'm warning you now, I want nothing to do with it. And, in my opinion, Gerald is totally incapable of murder. You've got it wrong this time, ladies."

Rachel and Marjorie laughed. Sarah generally saw only the good in people and struggled with the concept of anyone inflicting harm on another as a general principle. Her experiences as a nurse frequently challenged her inherent desire for world peace, but Marjorie had to admit, Sarah was usually an excellent judge of character – unless her faith in a person blindsided her.

"I'm sure you're right, dear. Anyway, hush, the interloper's on her way."

Marjorie was still chuckling at her own joke when Edna, who had clearly imbibed a decent amount of alcohol, helped herself to the seat Jana had vacated. Horace and Naomi Curtis accompanied her.

"Don't mind if we join yer, do yer, Marge?"

Marjorie let out an exasperated sigh as Horace made a beeline for Rachel.

"Mr Tyler, good to meet you again," she said, distracting him for a moment while Rachel pulled in another chair next to her for the bridal woman to take, giving Marjorie the thumbs up as Naomi sat down.

"Oh, erm, call me Horace," the man took his defeat with good grace, turning to his right. "This is Naomi Curtis, I'm not sure if you've met."

Marjorie smiled at the eye-catching woman while assessing her. Immaculately turned out in a floral cocktail dress with laced nape, Naomi wore an aquamarine pearl necklace and pearl drop earrings.

"How do you do? I'm Marjorie, these are my young friends, Rachel and Sarah."

Naomi's eyes glazed over. "Good to meet you all. Edna's been telling us about how you generously offered to share your suite when you found they had double booked hers. I'd have been furious."

Not quite how it happened. Marjorie shot her cousin-in-law a sideways glance, but Edna was too busy ordering another drink to notice.

Horace chortled. "Shame that Larry fellow stayed on board; you could have had their room, Edna."

Edna laughed or rather, snorted.

"I hardly think that's appropriate, Horace. The man's just lost his wife." Naomi tried to straighten up, although alcohol – Marjorie feared – prevented her from being able to do so with dignity.

"Well, he's hardly the grieving widower, is he? Glad to be shot of her, if you ask me." Horace turned on Naomi, who was about to protest. "Take a look for yourself, he's over there." Horace pointed an overly long finger, reminding Marjorie of a scarecrow, in the direction of a group not too far away.

Larry Mitchell was laughing and joking with three other men, and Florence Watson, the pet supplies businesswoman Marjorie and her friends had met the previous evening, was still with the company. They watched in silence for a few moments, astonished that a man could appear so happy on the day of his wife's death.

"See what I mean?" A triumphant Horace Tyler raised a glass of whisky to his lips.

"We all deal with grief differently," slurred Edna, knocking back what looked like a gin and tonic.

Marjorie felt a pang of sympathy.

"I don't think too many people will grieve the loss of that woman," Horace snarled.

"I thought you didn't know her?" Marjorie challenged.

"I didn't. Not recently, anyway. I think we might have had a bit of a fling years back – that's what she said, anyway. Can't remember – there were so many, know what I mean?" Horace winked at Rachel, who shot him a glare that Marjorie recognised as her famous 'in your dreams' look. Rachel had told her it had taken years to perfect.

"The one that got away, hey, Horace?" Edna teased.

Horace chortled again. "Hardly! That woman had no grace, and poison was her middle name."

"It seems you remember her more than you let on," said Naomi, looking like she was trying to blink away the fog from her glazed eyes.

"Not as much as you do, though. I saw you in a very heated conversation with her last night. What was all that about, then?" Horace retorted.

Naomi pulled herself up, supporting her weight with both hands on the table, and glared at Horace.

"Nothing. It was about nothing."

"It wouldn't surprise me if someone did her in," Horace said, ignoring Naomi's reaction. "People have been talking, you know."

Naomi swept an arm out to no-one in particular. "Enough of this. I'm going to bed, we've got an early start in the morning." Picking up her white handbag, she made a staggering rather than elegant exit.

"A bit precious, isn't she?" Horace sneered.

"Now look what you've done," complained Edna. "I like Naomi, we were supposed to be talking fashion. What is it with you lot? Why does it matter who knew or didn't know the Pruning Fork? She's dead, let it be."

"Edna's right. And makes a good point," agreed Sarah.

"Pleased to see one of your friends has got some sense in her brain, Marge," said Edna, shooting a disapproving look Rachel's way.

"Hey! I didn't say anything."

"You were thinking it, though, weren't you? I might have had a few, but I know a nosy parker when I see one."

"I'll thank you not to insult my friends while you are with me." Marjorie stood. "Time for bed, I think."

Rachel was at her side in an instant while Sarah said goodnight to Edna and Horace. Rachel burst out laughing as soon as they were out of the lounge.

"I'm pleased you think it's funny, I have to share a room with that woman," but Marjorie sniggered despite herself.

"Hardly a room," corrected Sarah. "Isn't she in the sitting room?"

"Still too close for comfort." Marjorie let out a slow breath. "It's funny, I was warming to her earlier – she's had cancer, you know. That's why she wears the wigs."

"I'm sorry to hear that," said Sarah. "Will she be all right?"

"I expect she'll outlive us all, dear." Marjorie giggled. "You are right, though, Sarah. I feel we should not let the death of Greta Mitchell ruin our holiday."

Rachel gave her a quizzical look. "If you're sure?"

"I'm certain."

"At last, some wisdom!" exclaimed Sarah.

"Goodnight, both, sleep tight."

"You too, Marjorie."

They each kissed her on the cheek and went next door to their room. As she stood with her back to the door after entering her suite, Marjorie giggled.

"Who are you trying to kid, Snellthorpe?"

Chapter 13

Marjorie lay in bed, mulling over the day's events and the evening's discoveries. She was certain malice was the cause of Greta Mitchell's downfall. It seemed odd that, despite their denials, so many of her old enemies were among the river cruise guests, almost as if by design rather than chance.

Others might not wish to dig deeper into the woman's death and, despite having only met her briefly, Marjorie could understand why. Nevertheless, if a murder had been committed, she would uncover the truth, this time without troubling Rachel.

Having made the decision to do some undercover investigating, she felt happier and settled her head back into the luxury pillow. Before she got the chance to drift off, she heard the door to the suite open and something fall over.

"Damn it!" Edna's loud voice cursed.

"Why doesn't she just turn on the light?" Marjorie muttered, irritated. She turned over with a sigh and pulled the covers over her head. Moments later, she heard the bedroom door open. *Now what?* She pretended to be asleep.

Heavy footsteps attempting to tiptoe around the room forced her to smile, soon to be replaced by a frown as Edna sat at her dressing table and switched on the light there. A loud whisper filled the room.

"Are you awake, Marge?"

How could I be anything else? Marjorie retorted in her head, but didn't reply.

Edna was obviously preparing for bed as drawers opened and closed. Humming was the last straw. Marjorie threw the covers off her head and sat up.

"Do you think you could make any more noise?" she snapped.

A startled Edna turned around halfway through makeup removal.

"Oh, sorry. Did I wake you?"

"And how did you imagine I would sleep through the racket you're making? Why are you doing all this nonsense in my bedroom and not the bathroom?"

Bleary eyes stared back at her. "I thought you might like a girly chat before we settled down for the night, but you were asleep."

Edna's sarcasm infuriated Marjorie, who glared.

"Look, I forgot to take my stuff out before going out this evening; it's no big deal, Marge."

Marjorie wasn't a violent woman, but she strongly resisted the temptation to throw something large and heavy at her unwelcome guest.

"Speaking of deals, what part of this behaviour constitutes staying out of my way and never referring to me by that ridiculous name? We agreed conditions, Edna, at least one of which I would remind you to heed from now on. Now get out of my bedroom before I call Faith Weathers and ask her to have you removed."

Marjorie's voice shook with anger. Edna hesitated, clearly weighing up whether or not to argue. She rose from the chair and huffed.

"All right, keep yer 'air on. I'm going."

"Interesting choice of words," said Marjorie, staring at the bald head of her cousin-in-law. Their eyes locked as Edna's hand went to her hairless head and they both started to titter softly. As the irony sank in, their laughter got louder and louder until they were both guffawing like a pair of teenagers.

Edna bent over double. "Oh stop, Marjorie, I'm getting a stitch."

Marjorie couldn't stop. As the tension left her body in a wave of hysterics, tears streamed down her face. Edna sat on the edge of Marjorie's bed, convulsing and holding her side.

Eventually they regained control. The streaks through Edna's half-removed foundation juxtaposed with the shiny head almost set Marjorie off again, but she managed to contain herself and reached for the glass of water on her bedside table before turning on the overhead light so she could see more clearly.

"I didn't have you down as a person with a sense of humour, Marjorie Snellthorpe."

"Well, life's full of surprises, isn't it?"

"It is that. Sorry for waking you, I really did forget."

Marjorie shrugged. "I see you've sobered up."

"Yeah. Me and Horace went for a late-night stroll around the deck. We had strong coffee and chatted under the moonlight."

"How romantic," Marjorie's sarcasm couldn't be disguised.

"He's all right, you know, Marge... erm, Marjorie. Underneath all the charade, he's quite agreeable."

"For a potential murderer." Marjorie regretted her words immediately, but couldn't haul them back.

"You don't really think that Mitchell woman was murdered, do you? I thought you were kidding."

Marjorie hesitated before saying, "It's quite a coincidence, isn't it, that she comes on a river cruise where she appears to have crossed paths—"

"Or swords."

"Quite. Or swords with several people? And I wouldn't be at all surprised if more than one of them wanted her dead."

"Horace did say he was pleased to see the back of her."

"I got that impression when you interrupted our evening."

Ignoring the dig, Edna replied, "Apparently, she threatened him."

"In what way? Do you mean blackmail?"

"Maybe. Dunno really, he wouldn't say any more. Just that he was glad she was gone. He's not a killer, though, and I don't think she was murdered at all. Maybe it was just fate: she spread dirt and malice, perhaps that's why she got her comeuppance."

Marjorie rubbed her right temple. "Hmm. Time will tell. Is there an internet café on board?"

"Don't think so, but I've got my tablet. I take it you want to look at her blog?"

"You're sharper than you look. I would be interested to see if anyone on board was a target of any recent articles, but I think I've had quite enough excitement for one night. It can wait until tomorrow."

Edna looked at Marjorie's bedside clock. "Blimey! We'll be in Cologne in a couple of hours. I'd better get some beauty sleep."

"Good idea."

Edna walked towards the door before stopping and turning.

"You're all right, you know, Marjorie."

"Goodnight, Edna."

"Night, Marge."

Just when I thought it was going well. Marjorie huffed, switched off the lights and settled her head against the pillow once more, drifting into a deep sleep.

Chapter 14

The telephone ringing in the sitting room woke Marjorie with a start. She checked the time and realised it would be Rachel wondering where she was. Scrambling into the dressing gown hanging in the wardrobe, she went through. Snores rumbling from the bed settee alerted her to the fact that Edna was still fast asleep.

"Hello, Rachel."

"Thank God! I've been worried sick, Sarah and I have been banging at your door for ages. What's that noise?" Rachel didn't pause for breath.

"I'll pop round and explain. Just a moment." Marjorie put the telephone down, pocketed the room key and, after checking the corridor was clear, scurried next door where Rachel waited.

Her friend's eyes opened wide. "You overslept! That's a first."

Marjorie hurried inside. "Good morning, Sarah." Sarah stepped towards her and kissed her on the cheek, frowning at Rachel.

"I told you she probably had a bad night and needed a lie in."

"You could call it that," explained Marjorie. "My house guest returned at some unearthly hour and made a terrible din. Once I was awake, we got talking, and the time flew, hence I slept in."

"At least you're talking," commented Sarah.

"I am sorry. Why don't you two go off and do the walking tour instead of our planned leisurely stroll? I fear it will take me a while to get ready and I need breakfast inside me these days before I can go anywhere."

"We can't leave you on your own," argued Rachel.

"I'm not twelve, dear. Of course you can. We'll meet up after lunch and I'll join you for a little outing then." Rachel opened her mouth to protest. "Don't argue, Rachel. I will be fine."

"What was that noise in your room?" Rachel asked. "It sounded like thunder."

"That, my dear, is Edna Parkinton snoring. At least she had sobered up by the time she got in last night, which was a plus. She's taken a shine to Horace Tyler, of all people."

"Watch out, Rachel, you've got a rival," Sarah teased.

"Oh, I'm gutted, but I'll try to live with the loss," Rachel mocked. "Men are so fickle, aren't they?"

"I'm pleased to see you've lightened up. Now, off you go, meet me back here at two."

Sarah took Rachel's arm. "Come on, mother hen, let's get you out for a walk." She winked at Marjorie. "She really needs a run; these river ships don't offer her a running track and you know what she's like. A gym and walking track aren't good enough!"

"Yep, I do need some exercise," Rachel conceded.

"Come along then, Miss Adrenaline Junkie. See you later, Marjorie."

Marjorie walked back to her room while her young friends headed towards the stairs and the exit. She sighed. It would have been nice to have gone ashore with them, but she had another project in mind.

Markus the butler walked towards her. "Is everything okay, Lady Snellthorpe? I've just seen your companions heading out."

"I'm afraid I slept in, Markus. Late nights and old age don't mix."

"Can I get you anything?"

"Would it be a bother to ask for two breakfasts, a pot of tea and a flask of strong coffee?"

"Give me fifteen minutes, Lady Snellthorpe."

"You can drop the Lady thing, Markus. Call me Marjorie."

Markus smiled. "Marjorie it is, then. I won't be long."

The amicable young German whistled as he went about his business.

Edna's snoring thundered through the room; it was almost melodic in a horrid sort of way.

"I'm going to need earplugs for when I'm less tired," she muttered before taking a shower. By the time she was dressed, Markus had reappeared with breakfast. When he brought in the trolley, Marjorie noted his wide eyes drawn to the raucous lump on the bed settee.

"Enlarged adenoids, I expect," she said, smiling.

"Should I open the curtains?" he asked.

"Oh, yes, please. It's high time my roommate was awake."

Glorious sunlight shone through the room once he pulled the heavy drapes back. Edna moaned and pulled the covers over her head.

"Thank you, Markus, I'll take it from here," Marjorie placed a generous tip in his hand.

"Thank you, Marjorie. Let me know if there's anything else you need."

Marjorie helped herself to grapefruit and poured a cup of tea.

"Coffee?" she asked.

"Mmm," came from under the covers.

Marjorie poured a coffee and left it to one side while she strode out on to the balcony to enjoy breakfast in peace. A few passengers she recognised waved as they navigated the ramp to portside. She watched an ambulance driving away and hoped no-one had taken seriously ill.

People were coming and going along the ramp, mostly going. Marjorie enjoyed toast and marmalade after her fresh grapefruit. There was also a plate of mixed meats and cheeses: a traditional European breakfast. Although she wasn't a fan of salami, she enjoyed the parma ham.

Edna finally appeared, holding a fresh cup of coffee, a brunette wig hiding the hair loss this morning.

"Good morning. I was beginning to think you were allergic to sunlight."

Edna squinted. "I might well be this morning."

"I hope you don't mind, I ordered breakfast for two, although the toast may be a little on the cool side now."

Edna plonked herself down on a chair and joined Marjorie. She picked up a slice of toast and slathered it with butter and jam.

"No problem, I'm starving." True to her word, Edna ate as if she hadn't seen food in weeks, polishing off the remaining toast, meats and cheese. Finally, she sat back to give her jaw a rest.

"I have to say, the food on board this vessel is second to none. I didn't get much sleep last night, always makes me hungry."

Well, you certainly made up for both this morning, remained unsaid. Instead, Marjorie poured herself another cup of now lukewarm tea.

"It's a beautiful day. Rachel and Sarah have gone ashore."

"I hope you didn't stay behind on my account," said Edna.

"No. I slept in and didn't want to delay them any further. I'll meet up with them this afternoon and we'll do a little exploring."

"The reason I didn't sleep well was that I was thinking over what you said last night about the Pruning Fork's demise. You know, Marjorie, you could be right about her being bumped off. Although shoving someone down the stairs may not have been premeditated, you know. It could have been a spur-of-the-moment thing. From what Horace told me last night, the woman could be pretty annoying."

Like someone else I know, thought Marjorie. "I'm surprised you remember anything Horace told you last night. You had imbibed large quantities of alcohol when you were with him."

"Oh come on, Marge. You make it sound like a sin. I'm on holiday, it's what people do when they're on their jollies."

"That's a matter of opinion. But each to their own."

"You can be a right snob at times, not to mention a prude. Anyway, I told you last night, we had coffee afterwards, which cleared the head – see, I do remember. He's a nice guy underneath the mouth."

"So you said. Back to the crime, or probable crime. I concede, it's possible the person – what does Rachel call them? Oh yes, the perpetrator may not have meant to kill her at all. It was rather unfortunate she landed as she did."

"Yeah, but shoving – if she was shoved – a woman of her age down a set of stairs would not end up with a few bruises, would it? I mean, if she was pushed, they meant to do her some serious harm, one way or another."

"I suppose they did. Whether murder or manslaughter, I'm determined to find out who is responsible. And I'm warning you, Edna, it could turn out to be your Horace Tyler."

"He's not *my* Horace Tyler. Dennis was the only man for me, but Horace's fun, and what's more, he's rich, so who knows? I might get what's due to me after all."

"Oh, don't start that 'woe is me' nonsense again."

Marjorie glared at her cousin, but seeing the twinkle in Edna's eyes, realised she was teasing.

"You said you had a tablet? I would like to take a peek at that Pruning Spade thing."

"Fork."

"Pardon?"

"Pruning Fork, not spade. Tell you what, why don't I take a shower while you have a read through? Then we can go for a bite to eat on shore if you're up to it."

Flabbergasted at her cousin's desire to consume more food after such a hearty breakfast, Marjorie shook her head.

"What do you mean, if I'm up to it?"

"Well, you are getting on a bit. Shouldn't you use a stick or something?"

Marjorie held her hand out. "The tablet, please. I believe it's time you went for your shower."

Chapter 15

With every story, Marjorie found herself strangely engrossed. How could anyone write such slanderous drivel about so many people? Did these people even exist?

The 'About' section of Greta Mitchell's website painted a picture of a woman wanting to tell the ungarnished truth about her subjects. The disclaimer, however, gave her licence to change names, places and what she described as minor identifying features. Marjorie suspected Greta's subjects were readily identifiable and that her 'ungarnished' truth was more likely garnished with lies and innuendo.

"Addictive, isn't it?"

Marjorie hadn't heard Edna come on to the balcony where she was straining to read the type in the latest article.

"In a masochistic kind of way, and if you like that sort of thing. It makes me feel I need a wash, and the things she says about her husband... well."

"You recognised him, then?"

"It would be impossible not to, having met them. She really was a detestable human being." Throughout the blog, Marjorie had noticed the repetitive snipes towards the boring and irritating husband of an imaginary woman called Mia. Greta hadn't even had the decency to change the man's name.

"Everyone who reads it knows she's Mia, the long-suffering wife yearning for excitement, but not getting it at home. Do you remember that piña colada song?"

"I don't know what you're talking about."

"*Escape (The Piña Colada Song)*, that's what it's called. I've sung it in pubs."

Marjorie had forgotten that Edna used to be a singer like her mother. "I don't believe I've heard it." She hoped her cousin-in-law wouldn't be tempted to give her a rendition, her head was sore from lack of sleep.

"It was about a couple who were bored with each other. I'll explain it one day, but back to the fictional Mia, aka Greta Mitchell."

"Are you suggesting boredom's the reason she resorted to writing?" Not waiting for an answer, Marjorie continued. "But talk about poison pen, or in her case, keystroke – she epitomises it. Was there anyone she liked?"

Edna was applying fresh polish to her fingernails as she looked up thoughtfully. "There's one man she refers to as suave, but then she refers to him as an unfaithful b—"

"Quite," interrupted Marjorie. "And I believe she means Gerald Banks there."

Edna's mouth opened wide. "Really? Whatever makes you think that?"

"Well, the suave man is black, for one thing."

"Marjorie, I hate to break it to you, but you do realise there's more than one black man in the world, don't you?"

"Of course I do," Marjorie snapped. "But the man she refers to as irresistible, funny and tempting, he also has a gullible foreign wife who works as a university professor."

"That could refer to anyone, and I for one wouldn't describe Jana Tipsarovic as gullible."

"Not in the professional sense, no. But what about in love? Many people are gullible in love." Marjorie thought about the conversation over dinner the previous night, the unfortunate secretary who had met the same end as Greta Mitchell. She suspected Jana knew there had been more to the secretary's relationship with her husband than she was willing to admit. "Besides, he knew Greta Mitchell."

"How do you know that?"

"The way he behaved when I asked him if he did at dinner last night. He denied it, but I'm sure he was lying. He was also at the top of the stairs at the time of the apparent fall."

Edna had finished with the nail polish, for which Marjorie was grateful as the strong odour caught in her throat.

"So you think he might have toppled her down the stairs? It seems a bit far-fetched; he and Jana seem very happy together, from what I can see. What did the article you think is about him say?"

"I won't bore you with the vitriolic detail, but suffice it to say, the man in the article is Oxford educated, as is Gerald, smooth and beguiling."

"I still don't know how you can be so sure it's Gerald Banks she's referring to. I remember the article now. Didn't the man's secretary die following a fall down the stairs?" Edna's jaw dropped as realisation dawned. "Just like…"

"Precisely. The facts speak for themselves. Gerald was forced to tell us about his secretary's 'accident' when Jana explained the reminder had upset him, his being so close to Greta when she fell."

"Now I see what you're getting at. You think Greta was writing about Gerald's affair with the secretary. It's coming back to me now, but I don't remember her implying the secretary's death was anything other than an accident."

"She stops short of saying so, but I believe the implication is beneath the surface. I've noticed she does that a lot in her writing – I can't bring myself to say articles – sets the scene, pours on the poison and leaves the reader to jump to her insinuated conclusions without ever saying as much herself."

"You know, Marjorie, you're right. I've often found myself arriving at judgements of the people in her articles without ever realising she was dropping breadcrumbs."

"More like boulders, but I take your point."

"So now we have to confront Gerald Banks and get a full confession."

"I don't know where you got the 'we' from, and I hardly feel confrontation is the correct method. I, or rather we – if you like – will quiz him further and see if he cracks. Shame, I rather like Gerald, but needs must." Marjorie handed the tablet back to Edna.

"Aren't you missing something else, though, Marge…" Edna held her palm up, "sorry, Marjorie? Look, it's going to take me some time to get used to it, all right? Anyway, aren't you missing the most obvious suspect?"

"Who is?"

"Her husband, of course. Horace told us he could have been driven to murder by that woman, and now you've read what she said about him. He has to be the chief suspect."

"But he has chosen to continue with the holiday. A guilty man would have stayed behind and played the grief-stricken husband, surely?"

"Whereas a slippery man might do the exact opposite." Edna snapped her makeup bag shut as if by doing so, she would convince Marjorie she was right. "Time to go ashore?"

Chapter 16

"Are you sure you don't need a stick?" Edna hollered from the portside as Marjorie took tentative steps on to the ramp leading to the shore.

"Take my arm, Lady Marjorie," the captain offered, much to the chagrin of Edna, who scowled. Marjorie gave her a triumphant grin as the swarthy man assisted her safely to land.

"Thank you, Captain."

The captain tipped his hat. "Have a good time ashore, ladies. There's an outdoor market just along that road if you're interested, or I could find you a guide?"

"The market will be fine. Thank you once again."

"Yeah, thanks for bringing her ashore, Captain. She's a bit unsteady these days."

It was Marjorie's turn to scowl. "You just can't resist being unpleasant, can you?" she remarked as they headed in the direction the captain had suggested.

"Stating the obvious, that's all. Perhaps the market sells walkers."

Marjorie harrumphed at the thought. "For your information, I'm quite capable of walking without any assistance. There is nothing wrong with my legs." To prove the point, she quickened the pace, leaving a breathless Edna trying to keep up.

"All right, Marge, you win. Slow down."

Tempted to go quicker, Marjorie pretended not to hear, but then remembered her cousin-in-law had had cancer not so long ago. She fought her inner pride and slowed.

"There you are. I thought you were fit?" The desire to have the last word on the matter was too strong to resist. Edna's cheeks puffed out as colour drained from her face. Marjorie stopped, allowing her to catch her breath. Struggling to speak, Edna leaned against a lamppost. Marjorie wondered if she had gone too far.

"Damned cancer. I used to be able to walk for miles," Edna wheezed.

"Would you prefer to head back to the ship?"

"No way. It's just residual anaemia from all the chemotherapy. I'm supposed to take iron…"

"Supposed to. Does that mean you don't?"

"They constipate me."

Not wanting to get into a discussion about Edna's bowel habits, Marjorie started walking again. Slower.

"I can hear people talking just along there. I expect it's the market. I'm sure we'll find somewhere to sit and have a bite to eat. You did say you were hungry."

With her colour returning, Edna kept in step and they found a bustling outdoor market in full flow on turning right at the end of the narrow road. They entered a large, cobbled square where five rows of stalls formed their own alleyways. The market was packed with shoppers and tourists.

"Over there, Marge." Edna pointed to the far corner of the square where tables were set up outside cafés. Marjorie would have liked to poke Edna in the eye for using *that* name again. A meander through the market would have been her preference, but the walk had demonstrated her companion's need for a rest. *It would help if Edna didn't eat so much*, she thought, but then chastised herself for being unkind.

They took the route around the outside of the market and headed towards a café packed with diners.

"Oh, look! There's Larry Mitchell with Florence Watson – we introduced you to her at the cocktail evening – and Faith," Marjorie declared.

"Who's the other bloke?"

"I don't know. Florence said she was meeting someone today. It could be him."

"Shall we join them and do a bit of snooping? Mr Larry Mitchell's still on my suspect list." Not waiting for a reply, Edna rediscovered the spring in her step and marched towards the assembled group. Her, "You don't mind if we join you, do you?" was loud enough to turn a few of the surrounding heads from people at other tables. Marjorie deliberated leaving her to it, aghast at the effrontery of Edna putting herself in charge of her investigation. But she acknowledged it would be churlish, and the lure of questioning Larry won her over.

"Do join us, Marjorie," Faith smiled warmly, clearly understanding Marjorie's dilemma.

"Thank you. It's such a warm day, I can't wait to walk around the stalls."

Larry didn't speak, but nothing would stop Edna wading in. "Sorry about your wife. I heard about the accident. Marjorie was there, weren't you?"

"Were you?" asked Florence. "Did you see what happened?" Her shaky voice suggested she was, as Gerald had inferred, a sensitive soul. Marjorie glanced at Larry, whose questioning eyes told her he would appreciate an answer.

"I'm sorry, I didn't see much at all. We were about to check out when we heard a commotion" – she omitted the scream, not wanting to upset Larry – "and one of my travelling companions, who is a nurse, went to assist." Pausing to check on Larry, who appeared frozen, she continued. "Unfortunately, there was nothing she could do."

"Where were you at the time?" Edna fixed steely eyes on Larry, subtlety not being her strong suit. Nevertheless, Marjorie was itching to know what he would say, especially as Gerald had told her Larry was in the vicinity.

"Greta insisted I check we hadn't left anything behind in our room, she didn't want our belongings going missing. An officer found me on my way back and informed me there had been a terrible accident. My wife had been rather clumsy lately."

"Funnily enough, she said the same thing about you the day we met," said Marjorie.

Larry swatted an annoying fly away from hovering around his partially eaten meal. "Oh well, I guess we both were. Must be an age thing."

Marjorie's brain tried to kick into gear. What was it Greta had told her? If only she could remember, she was certain it had a bearing on the death.

"I'm surprised you feel able to carry on with the holiday," Edna's feet-first approach marched on. "I couldn't do anything after my Dennis died. This is the first time I've been able to face doing anything like this. It's a year tomorrow since he…" Edna pivoted her head away, trying to hide the emotion she was feeling. The group went silent.

"It's what Greta would have wanted," Florence piped up.

"Oh? Did you know her?" Edna reengaged with the conversation.

"No. Larry told us last night over dinner. His wife was a stickler for routine and would have hated him giving up on account of her dying."

"I would have thought *dying* might warrant an exception from routine," snapped Edna.

Marjorie frowned, still struggling to remember that first conversation. Sighing, she intervened before Edna could say anything else.

"We all deal with grief in our own way. I'm so sorry for your loss, Mr Mitchell."

"Thank you," he had another go at the annoying fly, wafting his hand and almost knocking Faith's glass off the table. "It hasn't sunk in yet, if I'm honest. Continuing the holiday seemed the right thing to do, but…"

Edna was about to open her mouth again. Marjorie changed the subject.

"We haven't met your friend, Florence."

"Apologies, this is Christoph. I mentioned the other night he would join us for the rest of the cruise. Christoph, this is Marjorie and her cousin, Edna."

Cousin-in-law, Marjorie wanted to say.

Christoph's bright blue eyes reluctantly moved from Florence, but his smile was warm. "Pleased to meet you." There was a hint of a German accent. "I'm looking forward to the sailing." Then his love-struck eyes fixed on Florence once more.

"How did you meet?" asked Marjorie.

"We were just telling Larry and Faith before you arrived. Christoph's a progressive vet who also owns an animal pharmacy; he contacted me about some of my natural products. We met and became friends."

More than friends from his side, mused Marjorie, but she just nodded.

A waitress curtailed any further conversation as she arrived to take orders from Marjorie and Edna. Edna was soon distracted from her inquisition of Larry Mitchell, concentrating instead on tucking into a beef stew followed by apple strudel. Marjorie wondered if her insatiable appetite was also a side effect of the chemotherapy.

Larry, Florence and Christoph left soon afterwards, but Faith stayed behind. Marjorie wondered what it was like being a tour guide and having to spread yourself thinly among so many people, some of whom would be difficult to manage. Her eye was inadvertently drawn to Edna at the thought.

"Where's Daisy today?" she asked.

"She's accompanying a crowd on one of the walking tours, and Gustav is leading a bus tour. I'm just hanging around here in case anyone from our party needs help or directions back to the ship."

"Must be interesting, your job," remarked Edna, wiping away the remnants of strudel from her mouth. "How widely do you travel?"

"All over the world, although I tend to do Europe mostly. The long hauls are a young person's game."

"You're not old," snorted Edna.

"I didn't say I was old," Faith laughed, "but I'm the wrong side of forty, so I don't like to do too many trips involving twelve-hour flights nowadays."

"Still, you're not married, though, are you?"

Faith's right hand immediately went to her bare ring finger. "Not anymore, no."

"Divorced, then?"

Marjorie glared at Edna. "That's none of our business, is it?"

"All right. Keep yer 'air on."

Marjorie almost retorted it was time Edna used a different expression. The irony that had seemed so funny last night was wearing thin.

"It's okay. I don't mind," said Faith. "My husband took off with a woman he worked with. I was away a lot and I guess he couldn't handle it. We divorced on my fortieth birthday. He had warned me my job would be the end of us, so I guess I made my choice. You see, I love my work, it means everything to me." The slight squeak in the younger woman's tone took Marjorie by surprise. Edna persisted in her foot-in-mouth fashion.

"No-one else since? You must meet a lot of eligible bachelors in your line of work."

Faith's face flushed, and her eyes gazed into the distance.

"Well?" pressed Edna, impatiently.

"I don't suppose they allow tour guides to fraternise with guests in that way," Marjorie intervened.

"No, we're not," said Faith quietly. "It's a sackable offence."

And one you've been bitten by, thought Marjorie as she too stared into the distance. Was that the dirt on Faith that Greta had been going to tell her about? No doubt if she'd had knowledge of such a faux pas, Greta would have enjoyed divulging the information to anyone who would listen.

Marjorie sighed. *Another motive, another suspect.*

Chapter 17

Faith left Edna and Marjorie soon after lunch to help some other guests from their ship with directions. To Marjorie's relief, Horace appeared on the scene and offered to show Edna the sights. As soon as her cousin-in-law was out of sight, Marjorie took the fold-up walking stick from her bag, grinned and used it to support herself while she enjoyed a short traipse around the various market stalls, buying some souvenirs to take home.

After her shopping was done, she started the walk back to the ship to meet up with Rachel and Sarah. Faith appeared by her side.

"Are you happy for me to accompany you back?"

"I'd be delighted."

"Where's Edna?"

"Oh, she met Horace Tyler and opted to see some more of the city. I'm heading back to meet my young friends."

"Is one of them Sarah, the nurse who was so helpful yesterday?"

"Yes, and the other one's Rachel." Marjorie didn't mention Rachel's day job as she didn't want to spook the tour guide, although if Faith had done her homework on the guests, she probably knew all about them anyway. "Very sad about the death of that woman, Greta Mitchell. I find it bizarre that her husband's carrying on as if nothing's happened, but each to their own."

"It is rather unusual. He insists it's what his wife would have wanted."

"I got the impression you knew Greta. At least, she told me she remembered you."

Faith stiffened. "You can't believe everything that woman said, but we had met before. What exactly did she tell you?"

"There was a hint at some gossip. From what my cousin-in-law says, gossip, or rather character assassination, was her line. I can't imagine why anyone would want to write – or blog, as they call it nowadays – about other people in such a way."

"Me neither," Faith flicked her hair back from her eyes. She usually wore it in a ponytail, but today it was down. "I suppose she told you all about me."

"She didn't get the opportunity, and I'm rather pleased she didn't. I'm certain that whatever it was she wanted to tell me would have been fabricated."

Faith said nothing, as if weighing up whether Marjorie was being honest.

"But I suspect it had something to do with your marriage breakup and a relationship with a guest?"

"I'd rather no-one knows about it. Please." Faith's appealing green eyes settled on Marjorie's.

"As I say, I don't know the details, and it's not my story to tell, so it's not really my business. I thought she told me it was the first time she had been sailing, though. Was she lying about that?"

"I wouldn't know, but I wasn't working for Queen River Cruises when our paths crossed. Our meeting occurred when I did foreign tours for another tour company. The thing is, because of that woman, I lied on my CV when applying for this job."

Faith paused to take a deep breath before continuing.

"I met her and her husband, Larry, on a European tour about ten years ago; she seemed friendly at first. It wasn't until after the break was over I realised she had been ferreting out scandal on all the guests wherever she could. I remember now, she told me she had a fear of sailing because she couldn't swim. When I joined Queen River Cruises, I never thought I'd see her again and I'd forgotten all about her and the trouble she caused until I saw her in Amsterdam."

"Did she include you in one of her blog posts?"

"Oh yes. Not just that, a copy of it anonymously arrived at the tour group's HQ, and one was sent to my husband and Neil's – that's the man I fell for – wife. I wasn't lying about my husband's infidelity; it was finding out he was carrying on with someone from work that caused me to break the cardinal rule I'd set myself."

"I take it you and Neil broke up afterwards."

"It was not a relationship that was going to go anywhere, anyway. It only happened once, but Neil's friends told a few people on the trip, and you know how it is? Greta must have heard about it from them. I was foolish enough to believe it would all be forgotten after the holiday. How wrong I was!" Faith sighed heavily. "Once Greta published the blog post, me and Alan split up, but our marriage was over, anyway. Neil patched it up with his wife, but the worst part was, I got the sack from the job I loved."

"You must have been worried, meeting up with her again."

"Angry, more like, and devastated in the same measure. I hoped she wouldn't remember me and made sure I avoided her, but from what you say, she recognised me. In all likelihood, I would have lost this job too if she hadn't met her end like that.

"Work is everything to me. I had to build my career up again from scratch with the odd lie on my CV. My previous manager was sympathetic and gave me a good reference. When I clocked the woman who had caused so much anguish, I didn't know what to do. I opted for avoidance. When I saw the accident – you're going to think I'm evil for this – I was relieved; she couldn't continue on the cruise if she was in hospital."

"Were you near her when she fell?" Marjorie quizzed.

"Near enough to see her flailing as she took a tumble. I didn't want her to die, you understand?"

"Do you believe someone could have pushed her?"

"I've been asking myself the same question. If I'd been close enough, God knows, I would have been tempted to do it myself. I've been gathering from other passengers on the tour that she'd written about a number of them, too, in her thinly veiled fashion."

"Do you know who else she wrote about?"

"I'd better not say. I do still have some professional values to uphold, despite what I've just told you."

They were nearing the ship. "I don't believe one blot on an otherwise exceptional career should make you feel unworthy. You are exceptional at what you do."

"Thank you. Please don't mention this to anyone else, especially your... erm... cousin."

"Your secret's safe with me. My cousin-in-law's not my confidante, although she's not as bad as she first appears. By the way, did you see Larry Mitchell at the top of the stairs? I thought someone told me he was there."

"No. I spotted them on the way from their room – I was hiding behind a broad woman, and I heard Greta send him off like he said over lunch. If someone pushed her, it wasn't him."

"Good to know. I can't help feeling sorry for him, although I hardly know him."

"I tell you what, though, something had happened in the time between when I first met them and now. They were a doting couple back then. And despite finding out later how nasty she was under the surface, I thought she appeared much happier then. Still, that's marriage for you, isn't it?"

Marjorie didn't reply. Once again, she appreciated how lucky she was that she'd had a wonderful marriage to a man she still missed every day, and would continue to grieve for as long as she had breath in her body.

Chapter 18

Marjorie found Rachel and Sarah waiting for her in the sun lounge where they'd had tea the day before. They were glowing. A waiter hovered nearby.

"Hello, Marjorie. You timed it just right, we were about to order coffees. Are you having tea?"

"Actually, yes, but Earl Grey, please."

"Will that be ordinary coffees, ladies? We have some delicious specialities available."

"Perhaps later," said Rachel. "Just a straightforward, strong coffee for me."

"Me too," agreed Sarah.

"And one pot of Earl Grey coming up." The waiter swung in the bar's direction.

"You've both caught the sun. Did you have a pleasant walk?"

"We did. We joined Daisy, who took us all over the place. I feel like we saw the whole of Cologne in a few short hours," said Sarah. "She's great fun when she's out, same sense of humour as Rachel. Jana and Gerald were on the same walking tour. Gerald was in excellent form, obviously recovered from the shock of yesterday. And before you start again, Rachel, I don't believe he was having an affair with his secretary."

"I'm afraid he may have done," said Marjorie, telling them about the blog post she'd read that morning describing Gerald as a philanderer and implying the secretary's death was not an accident.

"That Greta Mitchell really was a nasty piece of work. How would she know about it anyway?" Sarah asked.

"I fear she, too, may have had an illicit liaison with Gerald, or at least wanted to. As the late William Congreve so eloquently put it, *'Heaven has no rage like love to hatred turned, nor hell a fury like a woman scorned'*, and all that. He said his secretary died about seven years ago, didn't he? Well, ten years ago, Greta and Larry had a happy marriage, but by the time the secretary died and Greta released the blog article about Gerald, they didn't. Something happened in between those years to cause Greta to create a character named Mia who was bored with her inadequate husband. Thereafter, the blog features a barrage of insults aimed at the man called – guess what?"

Their drinks arrived and were poured before Rachel answered.

"Larry."

"Precisely."

"Let me get this straight: you believe the Mia woman she invented seven years ago is really Greta Mitchell, and the man she insults is Larry Mitchell?" asked Sarah.

"Quite right. What I don't know is what happened in the preceding three years, except that it has something to do with Gerald Banks, who she initially describes as irresistible, but later turns on with the same venom she reserved for the other unfortunate subjects of her blog."

"How do you know they were happy prior to that?" Sarah asked.

"I walked back with Faith today and she had met them before, as Greta had hinted. I won't go into the details because I promised Faith I wouldn't, but she did say back then, Larry and Greta came across as a happy couple."

"No wonder Larry's pleased to be rid of her now, though," Rachel said.

"Nevertheless, he didn't push her down the stairs. Edna and I met him at lunch today and he said Greta sent him back to check they had left nothing in their room. Faith confirmed it."

"Ah, we know he didn't kill her," Sarah smirked at Rachel before taking a large gulp of coffee. Marjorie wished young people wouldn't drink as though they had just discovered water in the desert, but she was too intrigued to remonstrate.

"What is it you have discovered?"

"Well," said Rachel, "besides being great fun, Daisy's also a chatterbox."

"You were both right, as usual," conceded Sarah. "Greta was pushed down the stairs, but not by Larry, or by Gerald."

"So it was Horace?" Marjorie exclaimed.

"Horace? No, it wasn't Horace; it was Naomi Curtis, the wedding dress designer," answered Sarah, sullenly. "There goes my idea of getting Rachel to talk to her about bridal fashion."

Marjorie sipped her tea while trying to process what she was hearing. "Edna will be disappointed, she liked Naomi.

Did you find out what they were arguing about the other night?"

"Would you believe, wedding dresses?" Rachel forced a grin.

"No, I would not. Will you two stop behaving like children and tell me what you know."

Sarah finished her coffee and took a deep breath. "Okay, this is what Daisy told us. They found Naomi unconscious in her room this morning. It appears she took an overdose. There was a letter confessing that she had copied early designs of wedding dresses from Greta's niece, who had been at the same design school. Greta confronted her about it. Afterwards, she panicked, and finding herself at the top of the stairs with the woman threatening to ruin her, she nudged her. The letter says it was an extemporaneous moment; she hadn't meant to kill the woman, and she couldn't live with what she'd done."

"I saw an ambulance leaving shortly after speaking with you this morning," said Marjorie.

"Yep." Rachel took over. "That's when we bumped into Daisy, who was still in shock. We managed to get the story out of her when people dispersed during the walk. Jana seemed particularly relieved; I wonder if she suspected Gerald might have had something to do with it."

"So you were right about her being pushed, but wrong about Gerald," Sarah crowed.

"Fancy living a lie for all these years. Is Naomi Curtis dead?"

"We don't know. Daisy was ushered away once the ambulance arrived, but there had been a faint pulse when she checked. Anyway, they rushed Naomi to hospital. I expect we'll find out later."

"I wonder why Faith didn't mention it," said Marjorie.

"She didn't know. She left early to escort a group who wanted to visit the market, and Gustav had also left on a coach trip. We only managed to catch the walking tour because a butler calling for help delayed Daisy. She's the first aider for the cruise."

"I must admit, I wouldn't have suspected Naomi. I'm really not good at this detective work." Marjorie felt gloomy, but she also had a nagging doubt. Rachel would call it a gut feeling. "And you're certain it was her who pushed Pru Avenger, or Pruning Fork, as Edna refers to Greta Mitchell?"

"I for one am not certain of anything," said Sarah. "I didn't believe anyone pushed her in the first place, remember? I'm pleased Gerald's in the clear, though, even if he did have an affair with his secretary."

"We only have Greta's word for that," said Marjorie. "A woman who appeared to thrive on lies and innuendo. I wonder what happened to make her behave like she did."

"Who knows what makes other people tick?" Rachel said. "I've stopped asking. In my line of work, there doesn't always seem to be any logical reason. As for whether Naomi pushed her, the overdose and letter are compelling evidence that she did."

"Hmm," said Marjorie. Why wasn't she convinced? Was it pride at not having found the killer for herself?

Chapter 19

Marjorie returned to her room to change for dinner as the ship set sail again, heading for the Rhine Gorge and Rüdesheim.

Edna burst into the room, panting. "Where have you been? I've been searching everywhere for you."

Marjorie inhaled deeply. "May I remind you, we are not answerable to each other. Not now. Not ever."

"Oh, never mind that," Edna poured herself a glass of water, gobbled it down and opened the balcony doors, staggering outside to take in gulps of fresh air.

"Are you quite all right?"

Edna's face was bright red, and her eyes were almost popping out. Leaning on a chair to recover from the breathless spasm, she frantically pointed towards her handbag. Marjorie passed it to her, but Edna flapped it away with her hand, motioning for Marjorie to open it. She struggled with the strong clip, anxious that Edna might collapse at any moment.

"Should I call for a doctor?"

Edna shook her head as Marjorie finally won the battle with the clasp and held the opened handbag towards the distressed woman. Edna reached inside for an inhaler and greedily inhaled four puffs in quick succession. The colour returned to her cheeks and the breathing became less laboured.

"Why didn't you tell me you had an inhaler earlier when we were out? You should have used it then instead of telling me it was anaemia."

"The same reason you didn't tell me you had a fold-up walking stick." Edna's eye shot to the stick leaning against the chair inside the sitting area. "Pride."

"Hmm, touché. Shall I get us some tea?"

"I'd rather have a G&T," muttered Edna.

Marjorie poured a gin and tonic from the minibar for Edna and a sparkling mineral water for herself. "Are you feeling better?" She softened, wondering whether the other woman had told her the true story about the cancer being gone.

"Yeah. Ta." She took a large swig of the drink and closed her eyes momentarily. "The breathlessness is usually down to the anaemia, but now and then, particularly when I get over-excited, I get these wheezing spasms; sometimes I cough for England. The doctor gave me the inhaler for when they come on. It's an asthma-type thing. Never had asthma in my life. Damned cancer treatments are sometimes worse than the disease itself."

Marjorie remained sceptical. "Has the cancer really gone?"

"Cross my heart." Edna made the sign of the cross with her left hand, clasping the glass of gin in her right. "It's just left me with some health issues. Residual problems, the doctor calls them. I'd like to give him some residual problems," she guffawed and snorted.

Relieved to see Edna back to her usual self, Marjorie took the seat opposite.

"It's nice out here, isn't it?"

Edna's watery eyes took in the scene as the ship moved gently along the river. Blue skies made the view so much more scenic. She reached over and removed a packet of tablets from her handbag.

"See. Iron tablets. I suppose I'd better start taking 'em again."

"Yes, you should."

"The only thing is they give me constipation."

"You said. Perhaps you can have bran flakes and prunes for your breakfast."

Edna spluttered on her drink. "Old people's food, not likely."

"As you wish." Marjorie didn't want to discuss her cousin's bowel problems now any more than she had wanted to earlier. "So what was it you were in such a rush to tell me when you made your grand entrance?"

"Oh yes. I wanted to say we can butt out of the murder thingy. I know who did it—"

"Naomi Curtis," Marjorie finished.

"How come you know already?" A sulky frown appeared on Edna's face.

"Rachel and Sarah heard it from the young guide you terrorised on the first day."

"Daisy. She's all right, we've made it up. Even joined Horace and me for a drink this afternoon."

"Is that who told you about the Curtis woman?"

"No. Horace is in the room next door to Naomi. The butler came running out yelling and Horace went in to see what all the fuss was about. He saw an empty pill bottle on the floor and a typed note before Daisy arrived and shoved him outside."

"A typed letter, you say?"

"I think that's what he said. Yeah, it is. I remember now 'cos he said it was typed and signed like letters his secretary would draw up."

"Don't you find it odd?"

"What?"

"Well, here's a woman who is about to take her own life. She's distraught enough to down a bottle of pills, and yet calm enough to type and sign a suicide letter!"

"I don't know. Maybe she's the organised sort. The thing is, she confessed to pushing The Pruning Fork down the stairs."

Marjorie sat pondering for quite some time as the sun settled behind a hill in the distance. Edna tired of the topic having lost the element of surprise, so she nattered on about her afternoon with Horace, and then the people they'd met once back on board. Her voice rattled on in the background, but Marjorie wasn't listening to the words. It didn't seem to matter because once Edna got going, there was no stopping her.

"That poor young thing, she's had quite a time of it…"

"Sorry, who?"

"You haven't heard anything I've said, have you?" Edna giggled. "I think you're going a bit dotty in your old age. I was telling you about Daisy and how she tried to bring the pitiable woman round."

"By pitiable woman, I take it you mean Naomi Curtis. Is she married, by the way?"

"No idea. Why would that matter anyway?"

"One would usually spare a thought for those one might be leaving behind before taking one's own life."

"Well, p'raps *one* ain't thinking straight when *one's* about to top oneself," mimicked Edna.

"There's no need for sarcasm. Isn't it time one of us got ready for dinner?"

"I'll go for the first shower, I'm meeting Horace soon," Edna downed the rest of her gin and tonic and headed inside.

What happened to asking if that was okay? Marjorie sighed. She was not at all convinced Naomi Curtis was the killer, but to find out who was, she needed to check out that wretched blog again and speak to the few remaining suspects.

Chapter 20

Marjorie, Rachel and Sarah joined Gerald and Jana for dinner again. Edna was sitting with Horace and another elderly couple. Larry didn't appear to be in the restaurant this evening, so when Florence and her friend, Christoph, appeared looking for a table, Marjorie waved them over.

"Hello again," she welcomed the doe-eyed Christoph and introduced him to the rest of the group. The couple sat down between Jana and Sarah. Christoph nodded politely to everyone around the table. He struck Marjorie as being a few years younger than Florence and bore possible burn scars above his left eye, where there was only half an eyebrow. He had been wearing sunglasses earlier and she hadn't noticed it.

"How are you finding the *Amethyst?*" Jana enquired.

"It appears to have everything," he replied. "And the company is divine." He gazed at Florence, who didn't seem to notice.

Gerald was back to his captivating self, and he and Jana were as relaxed as they had been on the first night when they'd met over cocktails. They sparred friendly banter with Marjorie and tried to include the rather odd Christoph in conversation, with little success. He only had eyes for Florence, who clearly had something else on her mind. Perhaps she had picked up on Christoph's pheromones and wasn't interested, or maybe it was something to do with the deal they were brokering. The thought occurred to Marjorie that Christoph could be playing her along to get the business at a lower price. If that were the case, he was playing a superb role at appearing smitten.

As the wine flowed, the conversation became more animated, with Jana making everyone laugh. All that was, except for Florence, whose eyes, Marjorie noticed, had been fixed on the entrance all evening.

Marjorie's attention was brought back to the table when Jana mentioned the wedding dress designer.

"Terrible thing about Naomi Curtis."

"I can't believe it," said Gerald. "She was so talented. Why would she need to steal someone else's design, and why would she care what the Mitchell woman had to say about it after all these years?"

Jana squeezed his forearm. "Reputation is everything in that line of business, surely? Questions would start to be asked about other designs and more people would come out of the woodwork making claims – with or without justification. Before you know it, they would surround her with litigation."

Gerald stroked his chin. "I suppose so, but it's such a tragic waste of life."

"If what you say is right, she might still face claims. She's not dead," announced Sarah.

All heads shot in Sarah's direction. "That's splendid news!" Jana said.

"Fancy being driven to attempt such an awful thing. I understand the dead woman got under a lot of people's skin

– I don't know how a nice man like Larry ever got shackled to her." Florence's voice was shaky. "I was only speaking to Naomi the other night, so talented."

"My brother – he's a fashion designer – loves her work," Gerald agreed.

"I know, I love her designs. I've been looking up some more of them on the internet," Sarah added.

"Is she conscious?" Florence asked.

"Alas, no, she's in an induced coma at present, so it's not clear whether she'll recover fully."

Marjorie observed Gerald's reaction and was convinced there was a sigh of relief. Florence looked as though she might burst into tears at any moment. What was the matter with her this evening? Highly strung, it appeared.

"How do you know all this anyway, Sarah?" Marjorie quizzed.

"How do you think? Miss Marple here had to find out, so we checked with Daisy before calling for you this evening."

"You were just as interested as I was, don't blame me," Rachel protested.

"Rachel's a detective, she just can't keep her nose out of anything to do with suspicious deaths. Correction: she can't keep her nose out of crime – full stop."

There was a stunned silence following Sarah's revelation. The banter had gone too far and their ace card had been played too early, Marjorie felt. She watched the reactions around the table.

Rachel laughed. "Sarah exaggerates, I have nothing to do with murder inquiries. I'm just a plain old cyber-crime desk jockey."

Sarah's eyebrows furrowed, but she took the hint and said nothing further.

"Thank goodness. I'd hate to think we were all on some suspect list," Jana laughed.

"Not unless you have a laptop with you," Marjorie tried to sound jocular.

Christoph suddenly appeared fascinated by Rachel and asked about her work. Florence returned to checking the entrance every two minutes, and Marjorie was pleased when they had both finished their coffees and went their separate ways, along with Gerald and Jana.

Almost as soon as they were out of earshot, Sarah took Rachel's arm. "I'm so sorry, I think the wine's stronger than I'm used to. I would never have said anything if I thought there was still a killer out there."

"Don't worry about it, no harm done. Naomi's already confessed, so it shouldn't make any difference. It's just people behave weird when they know I'm a copper."

"Either that or they want to know the nitty gritty about what you do. That Christoph seemed quite interested."

"Yep, his questions were getting a bit too technical for me. I was pleased dinner was done."

"Why didn't you want them to know you were in homicide?" Sarah asked.

Rachel shrugged. "Because I don't want them to be uneasy, especially when there's been a homicide."

"And we're not certain Naomi is our killer, are we?" Marjorie caught the warning glint in Rachel's eye as Sarah reacted.

"You've got to be kidding me? The woman confessed and tried to kill herself. What more evidence do you need?"

"Sarah's right, Marjorie. This time it's done and dusted. I'm pleased Naomi Curtis is going to be all right, though. Sarah was so set on her designing my wedding dress." Rachel laughed as Sarah punched her in the arm.

Marjorie felt disappointment; Rachel was usually so astute. Surely she could sense there was more to this death than a petty disagreement over who designed what in the fashion world? Then Marjorie wondered if she might be wrong in assuming Naomi wasn't the killer. She wanted to mention the typewritten suicide note, but knowing how much Sarah had been looking forward to this holiday, she didn't want to spoil it for her.

If it wasn't for Rachel's past insistence and dogged determination to follow her own gut instinct even when things appeared neatly wrapped up, Marjorie would have accepted the conclusion already drawn, with everything pointing to Naomi. But no, there was someone else involved in Greta Mitchell's death, and Marjorie was going to find out who that someone was, with or without Rachel's help.

Chapter 21

Edna enjoyed Horace's company, but wished they were sitting with Marjorie and her young friends who seemed to be having so much fun. She liked Jana and wanted to get to know her better, especially as she'd been so friendly from the outset. Horace was all right, but tended to be a bit too full of himself.

Marjorie was growing on her as well, although Edna hated to admit it. She showed more of a sense of humour than during their previous meetings. Edna realised now that was mostly her fault; she had been so bitter, watching her mum struggle to get by while the Snellthorpes had everything. Her dad was a Snellthorpe, but she was beginning to acknowledge what a waster he'd been, and it made her feel differently about things.

Besides, none of this was Marjorie's doing. She had been wealthy in her own right long before she'd met Ralph Snellthorpe, and she'd tried to be friendly when they had met in the past. It was that row with Ralph that had really sealed their fate. Edna had been so embarrassed afterwards at her own behaviour that she'd cut off all ties with the family. Although Marjorie hadn't mentioned it, it was there, simmering under the surface. Edna was under no illusion that it wouldn't come up if she made a wrong move; there was no way Marjorie had forgotten it.

"What did you say your late cousin did for a living?" Horace asked, cutting through her rumination.

"All I know is he ran an extensive manufacturing business. Building supplies, I think. Why?"

"No reason, just curious. And your late husband? What did he do?"

"He was a senior manager over sales reps for a medical supplies company. They sold ventilators to the health service."

"Expensive equipment, I should imagine."

"I believe it was. He worked his way up from being a junior rep." Edna had been proud of Dennis, but she couldn't remember ever telling him so. She groaned inwardly. "How come you're still working at your age?"

It was Horace's turn to groan. "Nothing else to do. My wife died twenty years ago. I'd hoped the boys would take over the business, but I'm afraid we spoiled them. They are workshy, and to be honest, don't have the respect of the board. I'll have to retire one day, of course. Before that day comes, I'll sell up."

"Why don't your sons have the respect of the board?"

"Too damned rude. I know I can be self-absorbed, but they are totally selfish." Horace coughed. "We don't see eye to eye on very much these days. I think they resent the way I treated their mother. I had flings, you see, one of them with that dreadful Mitchell woman."

"I thought you said you couldn't remember her."

"I lied. I remember all too well. It was after my younger son was born; Harriet suffered postnatal depression, and I'm ashamed to say I couldn't deal with it."

"So you played away."

"Greta was a looker back then, and a real flirt. I succumbed. She wasn't married at the time, and it didn't last long. I came to my senses – that is until the next time."

"You said she threatened you. What did she have on you that would matter now if your sons already know about your behaviour and your wife's dead?"

"Ah, that. Well, like your husband, I wasn't born rich. My uncle was a black market racketeer, and he lent me money to start up my business when I told him about it. He didn't have any children of his own, and he also saw an opportunity for himself. No-one knew about it, but Greta must have done her research and somehow found out.

"Gracious, that woman was poisonous; even my boys don't know about that startup money. Early on, Uncle Graham kept me afloat, but the awful thing was – and I still baulk at the thought – I had to pay him back by exporting some of his contraband alongside my legitimate exports. It was ten years before I felt I could stand up to him and tell him I wouldn't do it any longer."

"I bet he took it badly."

"You could say that. He threatened to expose me. Except by then I had grown up enough to realise that if he snitched on me, he would be the worse off and we'd both go to prison. I told him to go ahead and do it. I'd rather go to prison, even if it meant bringing shame on my family. Needless to say, he didn't."

"And what did you say to Greta when she threatened to report you?"

"I told her the same thing. I don't know how she found out, but I doubt she had any proof. She was just fishing, probably wanted to call me out in one of those dreadful pieces she wrote. It's funny, I didn't recognise her at first. I know the years have passed us by and all that, but she turned out to be nothing more than a two-bit gossip and a would-be blackmailer. Not the irresistible woman I knew back in the day."

"Did she threaten blackmail?"

"I didn't give her the opportunity. Told her to do her worst and I'd get my lawyers to delve into her blogs, see if they could sue her for libel. She soon backed down, believe me. Women like that do the fairer sex no good and are best put in their place."

Horace's smug grin convinced Edna he wasn't one to mess with. It also convinced her that he wasn't responsible for Greta's murder.

Ignoring the sexist remark with some difficulty, she asked, "Do you think Naomi's suicide could have been staged?"

Horace scrunched his forehead. "Wow! You jump about a bit, don't you? How did we get there?"

"Never mind about that. Do you or don't you?"

"No, although the typed letter struck me as odd."

"That's what Marjorie says. I liked Naomi, so if someone did set it up, I'd like to find out who. Are you interested?"

"You mean do a bit of detective work?"

"Yeah."

"Even if you're on to something, I wouldn't know where to start. Neither would I be inclined to delve into other people's lives. Greta Mitchell got what was coming to her. I say good riddance. I'll drink to it, but I don't care enough to get involved."

"Don't you care that someone might have killed Naomi?"

"From what I gather, other than the matter that the letter was typed, you have no evidence to say that anyone other than Naomi tried to kill Naomi. And I say tried, because she's still alive, albeit in a critical condition, from what I hear. Daisy was checking her room, looking for something, so I asked her."

Edna's head shot up. "What was Daisy looking for in her room?"

Horace scratched his head before twirling his right earlobe, an annoying habit Edna had picked up earlier in the day. "Can't say I know. I didn't ask. Probably some paperwork she needed for the tour company, or perhaps she left her first aid kit behind. Who cares?"

I care, thought Edna. *I care very much. I'll show Marjorie who's the sleuth around here.*

Chapter 22

Marjorie left Edna snoring and joined Rachel and Sarah in the upper sun lounge to enjoy the spectacular views as they sailed slowly through the Rhine Gorge. Gustav was on hand to point out the many landmarks along the way through the World Heritage Site as they passed castles, churches and quaint villages.

"We're so lucky with the weather," exclaimed Sarah. "It's been beautiful, so far. Oh look, Rachel! There's Loreley Rock, I was telling you about it." Sarah, a keen amateur photographer, hurried outside with her camera hanging around her neck; this was heaven for her. Marjorie gazed at the large rocky outcrop that Gustav told them extended for 200 metres.

"I'd better go and check she doesn't fall over the side," laughed Rachel.

"You do that. I'm debating whether I should wake Edna, she's missing it."

Rachel smiled. "If I didn't know better, I'd think you were warming to your cousin-in-law."

Marjorie huffed. "Thankfully, you do know me better. I just don't want her moaning all day that I let her miss out on the views. At least she was quieter last night when she came in."

"She's larger than life, that's for sure," said Rachel. "I don't see why you should be her babysitter, though."

"Me neither, but she's been through a tough time. A lot of the bluster is bravado. I'll probably find she's up and out with Horace somewhere."

Rachel raised an eyebrow. "Well suited, those two. Okay, see you back here."

Marjorie was pleased to find she had guessed right when she got back to the suite: Edna was nowhere to be seen, leaving her to get on with further research. Marjorie checked the safe; the tablet wasn't there.

"Blast! Now what?" She opened the balcony doors to let air in. Moments later, she was delighted to spy the tablet on the table next to an empty breakfast tray.

"I can't believe that woman leaves it out in the open. Still, at least it's here."

Taking the precious cargo with her on to the balcony, she entered the passcode from a sticker on the inside of its case.

"I really must speak to Edna about security," she muttered.

Forty-five minutes later, Marjorie had just about worked out the where's and whys of the two crimes and narrowed down her suspect list. There were blog posts about the passengers she'd expected to find on the Pruning Fork's hit list. Gerald, she already knew about, but didn't believe he was involved. She was certain the killer was familiar with all the blog posts and had done their homework so as to make Greta's death similar to that of Gerald's secretary, just in case the police suspected it wasn't an accident.

The more she delved, the more convinced she was Greta's death was premeditated murder. There was the article about Faith (under an unfamiliar name), the workaholic tour guide who slept around with guests. It disgusted Marjorie that Greta Mitchell could weave such a pack of lies based on one silly mistake.

Poor Faith, I wonder if she's actually read this.

When she found an article citing accusations about a famous bridal-wear designer allegedly copying her early designs from the fictional Mia's niece, Marjorie was more convinced than ever that Naomi had done nothing wrong; neither had she tried to commit suicide. A quick internet search showed how easy it was to find Naomi Curtis's signature as it appeared on all her designs.

"How reckless people are when it comes to their privacy," Marjorie spoke out loud.

The answer came when she did a little more digging in relation to the so-called downtrodden Mia. Everything was there for anyone willing to pay due diligence. All she had to do now was prove who the murderer was, and for that she would need to speak to Daisy.

She scribbled a note to Edna and set off on her mission.

***

Edna and Horace walked along the outside of the ship, marvelling at the views along the Rhine Gorge. The ship was docked at their next stop, Rüdesheim, where they would take a cable car up to the Niederwald Monument later to enjoy even more spectacular views.

Horace suddenly spoke up. "I've been giving some thought to your idea that Naomi's suicide could have been a non-suicide."

"My cousin-in-law's idea, but go on."

"Yesterday morning, I heard someone knocking at her door. I'd forgotten about it because I was in a hurry to get ready to go out."

"Wasn't it the butler? You said he yelled for help."

"No. It was an hour earlier; in all the kerfuffle with the butler and everything, it slipped my mind. I don't know about you, but sometimes I can't remember what I had for breakfast."

Edna gasped. "You're saying someone visited her an hour before they found her unconscious? Didn't you think that was kind of important?"

Horace scratched his head. "I can't be certain it was her room. I haven't told you and I'm sure you haven't noticed, but I wear hearing aids. It can distort sounds, it's probably nothing."

"Did you happen to hear a typewriter while you were at it?" Edna snapped.

"Now you're being silly. No-one uses typewriters these days, they use computers."

Edna's mouth dropped open. "You're right – of course they don't and there would need to be a printer. Did you see a computer or a printer when you were in the room?"

"Can't say I did, I was too busy looking at the poor woman lying on the bed. I only noticed the note because it was lying next to her."

"Convenient, that."

"I'm not an expert in suicide, but I wouldn't have thought it unusual. People do usually like to explain why they are taking their own lives. At least, in all the detective programmes I've seen, they do."

"Come on. We need to find Daisy." Edna set off at a pace. Marjorie's friends stopped her in her tracks.

"Hello, is Marjorie not with you?" the blonde one called Rachel asked.

"Why should she be with me? You know as well as I do that I have to stay out of her way."

A frown crossed over Rachel's brow. "She went back to the suite to look for you. It was at least an hour ago. We thought perhaps you had gone for lunch together."

"I expect she's nodded off. She's getting on a bit, you know, probably can't keep up with you young 'uns."

Rachel pushed past her and Horace. "Come on, Sarah. Something's not right."

"Blimey! Talk about overreacting, or what?" complained Edna.

"Shouldn't you go with them?" Horace asked.

"What for? Anyway, look, there's Daisy. We need to ask her what she found in that room. Oy, Daisy! We need to talk to you."

Daisy's smile disappeared as Edna descended, followed by Horace. The passengers she had been speaking to excused themselves.

"Is there something wrong?"

"Not yet. We just want to ask you a few questions about yesterday morning."

"Okay. Shall we step inside?"

Edna noticed a few heads turning their way. "Yeah, let's go in there." She nodded to the bar. "I'll have a G&T, Horace, if you're buying," she said.

"Can I get you anything while I'm at it?" Horace asked Daisy.

"Orange and lemonade, please. It's hot outside. Are you going on the cable car later?"

"Yes we are, as a matter of fact," said Horace.

"Never mind about that now. This is important." Edna glared at Horace to get the drinks. "We'll be over there," she nodded to a quiet table.

Daisy looked fearful as they sat down. Horace appeared in double-quick time with the drinks, clearly not wanting to miss out on the interrogation.

"What would you like to ask?" Daisy said nervously.

"First of all, did you see a computer and a printer in Naomi Curtis's room yesterday morning? And second, why did you go back later?"

"There wasn't a computer, but there was a tablet. That's the reason I went back, actually. Word came from the hospital that her husband had asked where it was. They had called him to see her, and he couldn't believe she would attempt suicide. When he saw the note, he said it didn't sound like her. I handed the tablet over to the authorities before we left Cologne last night."

"And the printer?"

"There was no printer."

Edna and Horace exchanged a glance. "Thank you, Daisy. No more questions."

"You don't believe she tried to kill herself, do you? I don't think the authorities do, either, because no-one's allowed in the room now."

"Hmm. Interesting. Come on, Horace, I want to grab my handbag before we go ashore. We can tell Marge later what's going on. She'll be unbearable now, knowing she was most likely right about the Naomi thing. Still, I for one am pleased Naomi's not a fraud. I'm usually a good judge of character."

"Have a good time. I might see you up at the Niederwald Monument," called Daisy.

Edna waved a dismissive hand back at the young woman.

Chapter 23

Marjorie bumped into Daisy in the sun lounge shortly after the ship docked. "Have you seen Rachel and Sarah, my travelling companions?"

"No, I haven't, sorry. A lot of people have gone ashore to get the train to the museum or the cable car up to the monument. Faith's gone ahead, she'll be up at the monument now. Perhaps they left already."

"I don't think they would go ashore without me." Marjorie spied Florence and Larry heading in the direction of the cable car, and others she recognised going in the same direction.

"I saw Edna. She's with Horace; I think they said they were going up to the monument later," Daisy added.

"Right. I'll go on ahead, then. If you do see my friends, will you tell them I'm going up to the monument?"

Daisy smiled. "Of course."

"Oh, I almost forgot. I wanted to ask you how Naomi Curtis is and whether they found out what it was she had taken?"

"A lot of people are interested in Naomi today. I've had more questions about her this morning than anything else. She's still in a coma," Daisy lowered her voice. "Between you and me, they are having trouble identifying the substance she took, and we're getting a visit from the police later today. They want to search through her room."

"I see." Marjorie paused for a moment. "Who else has been asking about her?"

"Your roommate for one. Also, the Bankses enquired after her health, as did Greta Mitchell's husband. If I were him, I wouldn't want to know how my wife's murderer was."

"Quite. Well, I'd better be off, I need to speak with someone. Remember to tell my friends where I've gone, won't you?"

"I will. Enjoy the views up there. There's also a restaurant you might like to visit..."

Daisy's voice faded into the distance as Marjorie set off on her mission. She would have liked to chew over the clues she'd discovered with Rachel, but that would have to wait; she didn't want to miss the opportunity to solve the case before the police got involved.

The cable cars only had room for two people, so Marjorie waited for a lone traveller. She ended up taking the steep ride with a friendly teenager whose parents took the car behind, the spectacular views over the Rhine and the vineyards soon replacing any fears she had about how to approach the next stage of her plan.

The magnificent ride was over in five minutes, and once at the top, Marjorie scanned the area, checking to see if Rachel and Sarah were up there. Deep down, she knew they would not have come up without her, which made her feel guilty about not waiting to find them.

"Hello, Marjorie." Faith's welcoming smile soothed her pounding heart. "The monument's a brief walk over that way." The personable woman pointed toward the crowds.

"Thank you. I don't suppose you've seen Rachel and Sarah up here?"

"No, they're not here. I've been here almost from the moment we docked. There are some benches over there to the left if you'd rather wait for them, or the restaurant is a bit further down the hill."

"I'll take a stroll towards the monument. Have you seen Larry Mitchell, by any chance?"

"Yes. He and Florence Watson have gone for a wander over that way until the crowds die down." Faith nodded her head away from the amassing company.

"What an excellent idea, I fancy I might do the same."

Marjorie decided it was a good time to make use of her stick, so she removed it from her handbag and ambled in the direction Faith had indicated. It wasn't long before she came across Larry and Florence, meandering arm in arm along a quiet track through a luscious vineyard. Their laughter rang through the air, but it didn't disturb the birdsong; the birds were obviously used to humans entering their tranquil surroundings.

Marjorie hesitated. This was off the beaten track and most likely not the place for a confrontation. *Still, I'm here now, so I might as well get on with it.*

"Good afternoon."

Her call startled the couple who rounded hastily. Did Florence's eyes roll as she glanced towards Larry?

"Hello there," Larry replied.

"I'm pleased to have caught up with you. I wanted to have a word with you about your wife."

A frown clouded Larry's face. "What about my wife?" he snapped.

"I don't believe her death was an accident."

"That fact has already been established," said Florence. "Why can't people keep out of Mr Mitchell's business? Don't you think he's suffered enough?"

"I do, and for many years, I should imagine, not just over the past few days."

Florence's hard lines softened as she squeezed the man's arm.

"You're right there."

"Nevertheless, a woman has been murdered and another almost murdered."

"What do you mean?" Larry's frown deepened.

"I mean that the woman you have on your arm killed your wife and has tried to implicate an innocent bystander in her death, attempting to kill the unlucky woman in the process."

"Are you referring to Naomi Curtis as the innocent bystander?" Larry asked.

Why didn't he appear more surprised? "Indeed, I am."

"You're mistaken. She attempted suicide, from what I've been told." He blinked rapidly as if to shut out any other conclusion.

"And I don't know what you're talking about," stated Florence, pulling her arms from Larry's and folding them. "Why would I kill a woman I didn't know?"

Marjorie had to admit this was harder than she'd imagined it was going to be. Florence was putting on a good act. Rachel would be much better at this sort of thing.

"Because she kept you away from your father."

With the bombshell dropped, the reaction was now stunned silence.

Larry recovered first. "Florence wouldn't do such a thing. She is my daughter, you're right there, but my wife's death has nothing to do with her." But he sounded less than certain.

Marjorie remembered what she had been trying to recall for days: Greta had told her it was Larry's idea for them to take the river cruise. The pieces were falling into place. Faith had told her the Greta she knew didn't enjoy sailing.

"Whose idea was it to take a river cruise for your Golden Wedding Anniversary?"

Larry's eyes widened. "It was mine. Why?"

"Only yours?" Marjorie pressed.

"Florence suggested it would be an opportunity for us to spend some time together. I didn't know what had happened to her – her mother had her adopted, you see. We were only sixteen when she was born, and our parents insisted it was for the best. She tracked me down recently. I was going to introduce her to Greta, who didn't know I had a daughter."

This man was more naïve than Marjorie had imagined. "She had known for almost ten years. There were letters."

Larry's astonishment increased. "What letters?"

"Look, Dad, this woman's obviously an unhinged busybody. Let's go on with our walk."

"What letters?" Larry remained rooted to the spot.

"Did you never read your wife's blog?" Marjorie's voice softened.

"No. Why should I? She changed after she started writing that stuff – I heard enough criticism from her mouth, I didn't need to read any more."

"Well, she wrote about everything and everyone, including some gory details. It's not always easy to separate the facts from the things she made up," Marjorie glared at Florence. "She tore shreds off a pet supplies woman who she referred to frequently as an illegitimate *b*... I can't use the word. And more recently, she mentioned that this person was conniving to make claims on her husband to maintain her failing business. She made it clear she destroyed the letters. Tell me, Mr Mitchell, has your long-lost daughter asked you for money? Perhaps there's been a sob story to go along with the request?"

"That's none of your business!" Florence's nostrils flared and her voice rose several decibels. "Why don't you take your insinuations back to whatever rock you crawled out from under? Come on, Dad."

Larry didn't move. He rubbed his forehead. "Tell me none of this is true, Florence."

"Of course it's not. This woman is delusional." With gritted teeth, she turned to Marjorie. "I suggest you leave. You're ruining everything."

"Oh, you've already done that yourself." Pulling her eyes from the vicious stare of Florence, Marjorie turned to Larry. "I think you sense I'm telling the truth. Has your doting new daughter here produced any documents for you to sign money over?"

Larry groaned audibly. "They are in my room."

"Typed and printed?"

"Of course," he said heavily.

"So you have a printer with you, Ms Watson?"

"What of it? I told you, I'm on a semi-working trip."

"Yes, getting a new investor to pour finances into your failing business. The love-sick Christoph for one, but I don't suppose you need him now your... erm... father is investing."

Larry gawped. "You told me the deal fell through."

"Christoph wanted you to marry him, too, didn't he? But you were only interested in his money. And as for why I might be interested in the printer, Naomi Curtis's suicide note was typed and printed, and I doubt very much that she had a printer in her room. I don't believe *she* was on a business trip."

Larry's shoulders slumped. "But she signed the letter."

"And Naomi's signature is scattered across the internet, it's part of her branding. I'm betting her official signature is different to the one on that letter."

"Is anything you've told me true? Are you even my daughter?" Larry's tear-filled eyes stared hopefully at Florence. The rage in her face caused him to turn and walk back toward where Marjorie had left Faith. Marjorie turned to follow, but Florence bore down on her, grabbing her wrist and pulling her back. Her walking stick flew from her hand and Florence caught it.

"You evil witch. You'll pay for this." She spun Marjorie round and raised her right arm, wielding the stick. Marjorie closed her eyes, waiting for the pain to rain down on her.

"Oh no you don't." Just before she opened her eyes, Marjorie heard the welcome sound of Edna's voice, followed by a squeal from Florence.

Chapter 24

Edna held the struggling Florence Watson in an armlock whilst calling for help and gasping for breath.

"Can you manage?" Marjorie chuckled.

Rachel and Sarah arrived and Rachel took over, restraining Florence, who cursed and swore like a navvy. Horace appeared shortly afterwards, accompanied by Faith and a couple of men who introduced themselves as detectives.

Edna shoved her face a couple of inches from the now handcuffed and subdued woman. "I hope you rot in prison for a very long time. Attacking my cousin was unforgivable. Take her away," she commanded a stunned young detective.

"Yes, *Frau*. And who might you be?"

"Edna Parkinton,"

"*Danke*, Frau Parkinton." The young man mock saluted, and then he and his colleague led their prisoner away.

"Cousin in-law, by the way. Just so you know," Marjorie called after them.

"Oh, get over yourself," snapped Edna.

"I thought for a moment you were going to tell me to keep me 'air on," Marjorie retorted and both women giggled hysterically.

Rachel grinned before taking Marjorie's arm. "You had us worried when Edna found us and showed us your note, saying you were going after Florence Watson, the killer. We've been searching this vineyard for ages."

"You needn't have worried, I had it all under control."

Edna snorted. "Yeah, course you did."

"Why are the police up here anyway?" Marjorie asked.

"Edna left the note with Daisy, who showed it to them," Faith explained. "They found the printer in Ms Watson's room and came up here, hunting for her. Larry got back just as they were asking me about her and told them where she was."

"You shouldn't have come up here on your own, Marjorie," Sarah scolded. "That woman could have killed you."

"I realise that now. Had it not been for Edna, she would have. Thank you." Marjorie squeezed the other woman's hand.

"Anytime," laughed Edna, taking Horace's arm. "Told you she was in danger," she crowed.

"Oh, I forgot to say. The good news is that Naomi Curtis has come round and confirmed it was Florence who came to visit her yesterday morning," said Horace. "I overheard those coppers telling Larry."

"And while we're sharing better news, it seems we will be in a position to offer you a suite for you later on today, Mrs Parkinton. Once the police have finished in there, we'll have it packed up and cleaned. You can move in tonight." Faith winked at Marjorie.

"Really? That's great, that bed settee was getting on my wick, hardly slept a wink. Although I was getting quite fond of Marge," Edna laughed.

"If only the feeling was mutual," Marjorie muttered. "Now, how about some tea before we visit this monument we're all up here to see?"

***

Once in the restaurant a short walk from the terminus, they sat discussing events over tea and pastries. Marjorie explained how she had worked out who the killer was from Greta Mitchell's blog.

"She made it crystal clear her husband was gullible and needy because they'd never had children. Then about ten years ago – shortly after their initial encounter with Faith, actually – a long-lost love-child from his youth started writing to him. He never saw the letters, but the persistent Florence must have contacted him by some other means. Once she turned up claiming to be his doting daughter, he was smitten."

"Are you saying she wasn't his daughter?" asked Horace.

"He did have a child; he admitted he was only sixteen when he got the girl's mother pregnant and she put the child up for adoption. Florence could well be that child, or she could be an imposter, seeing an opportunity to take advantage of a lonely old man. I suggest we leave that one to the police, now I've solved the crime for them."

"If she is his long-lost daughter, it hasn't been the reunion he might have dreamed of when it turns out she's a lethal weapon." Rachel grimaced. "Poor man."

"Rather a pathetic man, as it turns out. So Florence's motive for getting in touch, daughter or not, was to get his money, then?" queried Sarah.

"It would appear so, and with Greta barring her way, she planned this trip to get rid of her. She must have realised people were suspicious and used Naomi Curtis as the fall guy."

"Any idea what she gave her?" Edna asked.

"I expect it was some concoction normally reserved for animals. She appeared to be quite the genius when it came to animal treatments. Whatever it was, she hadn't calculated it quite well enough to do away with a human being."

"I feel guilty about using her stuff on Pickles now," said Sarah.

"Her late cat," Marjorie explained to the confused-looking Edna and Horace. "Christoph was the backup plan if her sought-after dad didn't come up with the goods. She didn't bank on him falling in love with her. Utterly ruthless."

"I thought she told us she was selling the business."

"She changed her story later when Edna and I met her at the market in Cologne. That was the first hint that she might not be all she was pretending to be."

After they had finished eating, Edna got up to leave with Horace. "Well, Marge, I've had a ball. See you around the ship – sailing and sightseeing's gonna be boring after the past few days."

"Really? I'm rather looking forward to the peace."

"You know what, Marge? We must do this again." Edna smirked.

"Not on your life!" exclaimed Marjorie, inwardly smiling.

Rachel put her arm around Marjorie's shoulder after Edna left. "I do believe you've found a new travelling companion."

"Humph!" said Marjorie. "Now, how about some more tea?"

THE END

Author's Note

Thank you for reading *Death of a Blogger*, a novella prequel to the brand new Lady Marjorie Snellthorpe Mystery series. If you have enjoyed it, please leave an honest review on Amazon and/or any other platform you may use.

I hope you had fun meeting Lady Marjorie and her friends, Rachel Prince and Sarah Bradshaw. To find out where it all began, check out the Rachel Prince Mystery series.

The first book in the new series featuring Lady Marjorie and her cousin-in-law, Edna Parkinton will be available in the autumn of 2021.

A Cruise to Murder

Chapter 1

"I can't do this anymore, Rachel. I've met someone else." The words pierced through her brain, like knives carving her in two.

Rachel awoke with a start, wondering where she was. The rhythmic chugging sound of a train on railway tracks reminded her immediately. Pushing the dream to the back of her mind, she looked around the busy train. The middle-aged woman with a teenage girl in tow, who had sat opposite Rachel at the start of her journey, had gone. She had been replaced by a younger woman with customary ear phones attached to her head and eyes glued to the mobile phone in her hand. A young man, presumably her boyfriend, was sitting next to her, reading a book and eating a sandwich.

Rachel noticed that the rather large man who had been sitting in the aisle seat next to her had also been replaced. An older man reading a newspaper was now beside her. Realising that she must have been in a very deep sleep, she automatically checked that her handbag was still in place. She had squashed it between herself and the side of the carriage when her eyes had begun to feel like lead and she realised that sleep was inevitable.

Reassured that it was still there, she took a quick look behind her to where the luggage compartment was and noticed her suitcase remained where she had left it. Vivid pink with white polka dots, it was hardly going to go unnoticed, even though it was now surrounded by other people's luggage. She had bought it to stand out and stand out it did.

Looking at her watch, she saw that it was now ten o'clock in the morning. She turned and looked out of the window, the sadness that had been wrenching her heart for weeks re-surfacing. Work had been busy, and she had pulled in extra hours to help dull the pain, but now she had stopped, it came crashing in on her again.

Blast Robert – get out of my head, she thought as tears stung the back of her eyes. Thankfully, phone-girl was too busy with her device to notice the tears.

The passengers around her were eating and drinking, so she assumed she must have missed the trolley service. Another hour and a half and the train would be arriving in Southampton. The smell of fresh coffee made her thirsty, and she needed to stretch her legs. Rachel decided to go for a walk and get some sustenance.

With an involuntary sigh that drew a sympathetic look from the man seated next to her, she excused herself and made her way through the train to the buffet car.

The train was now tearing through the countryside and felt like it was floating on air, except for the occasional shaking of the carriages from side to side. It was much busier than it had been at seven-thirty when she had first boarded in Leeds. The walk became an obstacle course as she fought her way past different-sized luggage overflowing into the aisles. She almost lost her balance as she moved through the carriages and felt the sway where they joined together.

Why did I agree to this holiday? She was pondering this thought when she finally arrived at the buffet car. Sarah had been so kind and sympathetic when Rachel had called her two months ago after Robert ended their relationship, leaving Rachel feeling broken-hearted and alone. She had been engaged to Robert for a year, but had noticed a change in him about six months prior to the breakup. At the time, distracted by assessments and not really able deal with anything else, she had put it down to the work strain they were both under and dismissed his moodiness.

Robert worked in Manchester as a police sergeant. They had met at a party and were immediately attracted to each other, discovering that they both went to church and were both in the police force. He had approached her while she was sitting with a group of friends.

"Would you like to dance?" It wasn't the best pickup line she had heard, but from the moment she looked into his dark-green eyes, she was smitten. It had seemed an ideal match, and it had been as far as Rachel was concerned.

Rachel had recently joined the force when they first met and was committed to staying in Leeds until her two years as a student officer were completed. Robert had been supportive initially, and when he asked her to marry him, she was over the moon. They agreed that she would look for work in Manchester once she qualified as constable.

That was before – this is now. Sorrow and pain coursed through her veins.

She bought herself a rather stale club sandwich and a cup of strong coffee and felt a bit better for having something to eat and drink. Grateful that she was not one of those people who starved themselves when they were unhappy, she was equally aware that she did not want to comfort eat and gain weight – especially being a fitness fanatic. Even she had stopped eating for a few days following the shock announcement from Robert eight weeks earlier though.

The memories once again invaded her senses.

She had gone to visit him in Manchester, and as usual arrived at his sister's house. Robert's sister, Louise, lived around the corner from his flat. She was a kind and patient woman with three children under the age of five and a husband who seemed to work all hours. Louise was committed to family life although Rachel couldn't help noticing she looked exhausted most of the time. Rachel sometimes wondered if her husband deliberately missed getting home early in order to avoid having to spend time with the children or help with chores. She'd convinced herself that Robert would not be like that, and they would live as loving partners.

At least we would have done, if he'd got over his moodiness and more importantly, if he hadn't met someone else.

Rachel had arrived late on that Friday night and only seen him briefly.

"I'll collect you tomorrow morning at ten. We'll go out for lunch and spend the day together." He turned away before she could kiss him.

Her time was limited as she had to get back to Leeds on Saturday night to work on the Sunday. Looking back, she realised how foolish she had been, missing all the warning signs; but she had been studying frantically to finish her police assessments while planning for the future, and she was madly in love.

Louise had seemed quiet and distant over breakfast on the Saturday morning.

"Is everything all right?" Rachel wondered if she and her husband, George, had argued. George had left early in the morning and, unusually, had given Rachel a hug before he went.

"Yes, fine. I just need to get the children ready for their grandma." Louise had busied herself in the kitchen for the rest of the morning.

Robert arrived at around eleven o'clock, an hour later than they'd agreed. He didn't apologise for being late.

"I've only got time for lunch," he said brusquely.

"Oh, that's a shame. I was hoping we could go into town." She was disappointed, but tried to hide it, naively thinking he must have been called in to work – not unusual for police officers. Although a staunch believer in people's rights to protest, march, and all manner of other things, Rachel did sometimes wish they would spare a thought for the police. The police had to give up their days off and time with families to maintain public order. Even the most peaceful demonstrations could erupt into violence if rival factions got over-heated.

Robert was quiet again.

"I've just got the one assessment left to do next week and then I'll be qualified. It won't be long before we can spend a lot more time together." Rachel tried to make the most of the time they had, overcompensating for his lack of speech by babbling on. They stopped outside her favourite café; the familiar smell of percolated coffee and baking filled her senses. She entered the premises happily, looking forward to a romantic lunch, but Robert seemed to move away whenever she tried to hold his hand.

"I missed every signal. I was blind," she later told Sarah.

There was the usual queue of people waiting to be served, and they waited in line to order lunch and coffees. Rachel ordered her favourite home-made beef and potato pie and was about to tuck in when Robert grabbed her hand.

At last, some sign of affection. Then she looked into his eyes with a feeling of foreboding. He stared at her with a coldness she had not seen before; she was looking into someone else's eyes – these were not the happy eyes of her fiancé.

"I can't do this anymore, Rachel. I've met someone else. I love her and I want to marry her."

He threw himself back into the chair and took a deep breath. At this point, he looked away.

Rachel couldn't believe what she was hearing – her stomach was in knots and her heart was racing. Beginning to feel light-headed, she opened her mouth but realised she couldn't speak.

Taking advantage of the fact that she was unable to say anything, Robert continued. "I've tried, Rachel, really I have. I met Jessica through an inter-church thing – we started doing youth clubs together and things developed from there."

Rachel saw a look in his eyes that had once belonged to her as he began to speak about this woman whom he had dared to give a name. Somehow, thinking of this person as *the other woman* allowed Rachel to feel angry; but thinking of her as Jessica brought her to life as another person who had fallen in love with a man. Rachel's man.

Flabbergasted, Rachel shut down and went into autopilot. She could thank her police training for this skill because it helped her to survive the conversation – and it had become a matter of her survival. Her hand felt sore, and she realised that she had been twisting her engagement ring round and round while he was speaking.

"I need to go to the bathroom," she said, and then she got up and walked straight out of the café. At first, she didn't know where she was going, but after about an hour she realised she was heading for the train station. Her mobile phone had rung a few times with Robert's ringtone, but she declined the calls and turned it off. She knew she was not being very adult about this, but her heart had just been torn apart.

How else should I react? she asked herself, angrily. Tears fell down her face as she walked, and she had to use every ounce of strength to stop herself from sobbing in the street. A few people looked at her as she passed by with embarrassed fleeting glances, but no-one had asked if she was all right.

Sorrow had turned to anger by the time she reached the train station – anger with Robert for doing this to her, and anger at herself for missing all the warning signs. She saw there was a train leaving for Leeds in ten minutes, so she sprinted to the platform.

Once on the train, Rachel had found a quiet compartment, unusual for a Saturday. She sat down and tried to take in all that had happened over the few hours that had been spent with Robert. Her happy, stable life had been thrown into turmoil, and she felt terrified of the fragility that overwhelmed her. The dark and devastating thoughts scrambling through her brain were totally new.

If only I had recognised the signs over the previous six months for what they were, the pain might have been a bit less and I might have been better prepared for what just occurred. She felt betrayed, angry, dreadfully sad; but most of all, she felt stupid. Her father had tried to warn her about long-distance relationships – not that Leeds and Manchester were that far apart.

"I'm sure it will all work out for you," he had said following her engagement. "But just be aware that people can change, and you haven't known him that long."

Robert had asked her father's permission before proposing in the traditional way, and he had given it without hesitation. Rachel's dad, Brendan Prince, was a vicar in Hertfordshire where Rachel had been brought up. Robert had joked with her later, saying that her father had warned him: "Don't you hurt my daughter or you will have me to answer to." They had laughed about it then, but now Rachel wondered whether her wonderful dad had seen something in Robert that she couldn't or wouldn't see.

I don't suppose he asked my dad for permission to break off the engagement, she thought bitterly. *How do I tell my parents?*

When she got back to her flat, she realised she hadn't let Louise know that she wasn't going to collect her overnight bag. She turned her phone on and saw fourteen missed calls and numerous texts from Robert, all of which she deleted.

There was a text from Louise which read: "*I am so sorry, Rachel, for what has happened. We only knew about it yesterday. Robert had kept it all to himself. Please let me know you are okay, I understand you will be angry and upset. The children send hugs and kisses.*"

Rachel replied: "*Thanks, Louise, I have returned to Leeds. Sorry to leave without saying goodbye, but had to get away and take it all in. Love to the boys.*"

She received a sympathetic reply, but they had not communicated since, except when Louise had sent a parcel with her overnight bag and a *thinking of you* card. Robert had tried to call a few more times, but she had not replied. He did write one letter, which still lay unopened in her suitcase. She might open it with Sarah.

If only I hadn't joined the police force, I would never have met Robert. She knew it was silly to think that way, but her head was still reeling from the shock.

"You all right, love?" A voice behind her brought her back to the present. She had been staring out of the window opposite the buffet bar and hadn't realised there were tears streaming down her face. She gathered herself together, looking up at the buffet car attendant.

"Yes, I'm fine, thank you," she replied. *Pull yourself together*, she chastised herself, and eventually made her way back through the train to her seat, after washing her face at the toilet sink.

Almost an hour had passed since she had left her place. The train would soon be arriving at Southampton station. Thankful that her seat had not been taken and that her luggage was still in place, she sat down.

Get a grip, Prince!

Books by Dawn Brookes

Rachel Prince Mysteries

A Cruise to Murder

Deadly Cruise

Killer Cruise

Dying to Cruise

A Christmas Cruise Murder

Murderous Cruise Habit

Honeymoon Cruise Murder

A Murder Mystery Cruise

Hazardous Cruise (Preorder Now)

Coming Soon 2021

Book 1 in the Lady Marjorie Snellthorpe Mystery series

Murder at the Opera House (Available to preorder)

Carlos Jacobi PI

Body in the Woods

The Bradgate Park Murders

Memoirs

Hurry up Nurse: memoirs of nurse training in the 1970s

Hurry up Nurse 2: London calling

Hurry up Nurse 3: More adventures in the life of a student nurse

Picture Books for Children

Keep in touch:

Sign up for my no-spam newsletter at:

https://www.dawnbrookespublishing.com

Follow me on Facebook:

https://www.facebook.com/dawnbrookespublishing/

Follow me on Twitter:

@dawnbrookes1

Follow me on Pinterest:

https://www.pinterest.co.uk/dawnbrookespublishing

Acknowledgements

Thank you to my editor Alison Jack, as always, for her kind comments about the book and for suggestions, corrections and amendments that make it a more polished read.

Thanks to my immediate circle of friends who are so patient with me when I'm absorbed in my fictional world and for your continued support in all my endeavours.

About the Author

Dawn Brookes is author of the *Rachel Prince Mystery* series, combining a unique blend of murder, cruising and medicine with a touch of romance. She is also author of the Carlos Jacobi crime series and coming soon is the Lady Marjorie Snellthorpe Mystery series.

Dawn holds an MA in Creative Writing with Distinction and has a 39-year nursing pedigree. She loves to travel and takes regular cruise holidays, which she says are for research purposes! She brings these passions and a love of clean crime to her writing.

The surname of her Rachel Prince protagonist is in honour of her childhood dog, Prince, who used to put his head on her knee while she lost herself in books.

Bestselling author of *Hurry up Nurse: memoirs of nurse training in the 1970s* and *Hurry up Nurse 2: London calling*, Dawn worked as a hospital nurse, midwife, district nurse and community matron across her career. Before turning her hand to writing for a living, she had multiple articles published in professional journals and coedited a nursing textbook.

She grew up in Leicester, later moved to London and Berkshire, but now lives in Derbyshire. Dawn holds a Bachelor's degree with Honours and a Master's degree in education. Writing across genres, she also writes for children. Dawn has a passion for nature and loves animals, especially dogs. Animals will continue to feature in her children's books, as she believes caring for animals and nature helps children to become kinder human beings.

Printed in Great Britain
by Amazon

26349103R00098